Her mouth was silk. Her lips satin.

His own only grazed, lightly, so very lightly, using all his self-control to keep it like that. His arms were around her waist, hands on the rounded swell of her hips. As Damos lifted his head from hers, he smiled, that same half smile he'd used on her as he'd taken her into his arms to dance with her.

His eyes poured into hers.

"You have no idea, absolutely no idea," he breathed, "how much I have been aching to do that."

Kassia was looking at him with distended eyes, eyes that had turned as silvery as her gown, with wonder in them, and more than wonder. Looking at him in such a way that there was only one thing to do—only one.

He kissed her again. And this time the lightness could not hold, could not withstand his own desire. Desire that she had inflamed from that first stunned silence as he had walked toward her, her hidden beauty finally revealed to him, desire that had been building, achingly, all evening. Dancing with her had been bliss and torture—

But now the latter was gone, and only the former could exist.

Julia James lives in England and adores the peaceful verdant countryside and the wild shores of Cornwall. She also loves the Mediterranean—so rich in myth and history, with its sunbaked landscapes and olive groves, ancient ruins and azure seas. "The perfect setting for romance!" she says. "Rivaled only by the lush tropical heat of the Caribbean—palms swaying by a silver-sand beach lapped by turquoise waters... What more could lovers want?"

Books by Julia James

Harlequin Presents

Billionaire's Mediterranean Proposal
Irresistible Bargain with the Greek
The Greek's Duty-Bound Royal Bride
The Greek's Penniless Cinderella
Cinderella in the Boss's Palazzo
Cinderella's Baby Confession
Destitute Until the Italian's Diamond
The Cost of Cinderella's Confession
Reclaimed by His Billion-Dollar Ring
Contracted as the Italian's Bride
The Heir She Kept from the Billionaire
Greek's Temporary Cinderella

Visit the Author Profile page
at Harlequin.com for more titles.

VOWS OF REVENGE

JULIA JAMES

Harlequin

PRESENTS

Harlequin®
PRESENTS™

ISBN-13: 978-1-335-93936-4

Vows of Revenge

Recycling programs
for this product may
not exist in your area.

For questions and comments about the quality of this book, please contact us at
CustomerService@Harlequin.com.

TM and ® are trademarks of Harlequin Enterprises ULC.

Harlequin Enterprises ULC
22 Adelaide St. West, 41st Floor
Toronto, Ontario M5H 4E3, Canada
www.Harlequin.com

Printed in Lithuania

MIX
Paper | Supporting
responsible forestry
FSC® C021394

VOWS OF REVENGE

Memories of happy holidays in the Highlands
with my family.

CHAPTER ONE

DAMOS KALLINIKOS STOOD beside the excavation's director, Dr Michaelis, looking out over the site, paying only cursory attention to what was being said to him about the work being carried out around them. He was not here because he was interested in Bronze Age settlements on this remote island in the Aegean—though the good doctor thought he was—and nor, indeed, as he had trailed quite deliberately, because the Kallinikos Corporation might be interested in sponsoring the dig. No, his interest was completely different.

His lancing gaze went out over the site's excavators, many on their knees in the dusty earth, inching their way deeper with trowels and infinite care, some going back and forth, taking photos of finds or carrying them, with even more care, to the tables set out under the shade of olive trees around the edge of the site.

So, which one was she? She wasn't one of the females on her feet, so she must be one of those kneeling. He'd never met her in real life, but the photos he'd had taken of her by his investigators were clear enough. As clear as the résumé they'd provided him with of her particulars.

Kassia Bowen Andrakis, twenty-six years old, English

mother, Greek father. The mother he knew nothing about, and cared less—the opposite was true for her father. Yorgos Andrakis was a very familiar figure to him indeed. He was one of Greece's wealthiest men—and one of the most unpleasant. Damos had met him enough times to have that reputation confirmed.

But he didn't care about his personality—only about his latest business venture.

And the means Yorgos Andrakis was using to secure it.

Damos's expression hardened. Well, Andrakis would not succeed. The company he was aiming to add to his acquisitions was, in fact, going to be acquired by himself. Cosmo Palandrou's freight, transport and logistics business was ripe for takeover. Despite Cosmo's inept handling of what he had inherited, resulting in strikes and disaffection amongst his badly treated workforce, which had led to client contracts increasingly being cancelled, there was a significant amount of untapped value in the business—once it had competent management at the helm.

Damos had plans for its expansion too—capitalising on the large number of currently under-exploited prime site depots, developing new markets and maximising the synergy with his own marine-based interests. Oh, yes, there was a lot about Cosmo's business that he wanted.

But so did Yorgos Andrakis.

Andrakis, though—as usual with all his acquisitions—wanted to buy it cut-price, so that when he broke the business up, as he would, for that was his way with acquisitions, plundering them for what he could strip out, he would maximise his profits.

Cosmo, however, was driving a hard bargain with Andrakis—he wanted more, and the 'more' that Andrakis was prepared to offer him, according to Damos's sources, was right here—digging in Bronze Age dirt.

Kassia Andrakis. The daughter Yorgos Andrakis was planning to marry off to Cosmo in order to get hold of Cosmo's company. The bride-to-be who would make Cosmo a son-in-law to Yorgos Andrakis. A win-win all round.

Except that Damos had other plans for Kassia Andrakis...

His eyes narrowed. He'd just spotted her. She'd looked up momentarily, wiping her brow with the back of her hand under the hot sun, before resuming the careful twisting of her trowel around something she seemed to have found. Yes, that was her, all right—it tallied with the photos.

He let his eyes rest on her a moment. Did she know of her father's intentions for her? If she did, she surely could not be a fan. No woman would be. Cosmo Palandrou shared Yorgos Andrakis's abrasive, repellent personality, and physically he was just as unattractive—overweight, with pouched, close-set eyes, flaccid jawline and a slack mouth.

No, Kassia Andrakis could scarcely want to be Cosmo's bride.

But there was something Damos was going to ensure she *did* want to be—something that would stop Andrakis's scheme in its tracks, leaving the way clear for Damos to scoop up Cosmo's company himself.

Because Cosmo Palandrou was going to discover that Kassia Andrakis was the very last woman he would want as his bride...

He turned to the excavation's director.

'Fascinating,' he murmured. 'Could we take a closer look, do you think?'

Kassia Andrakis was getting to her feet. In her hand, Damos could see, was a shard of pottery. The timing was perfect.

Damos nodded towards her. 'Is that something just uncovered?'

Without waiting for an answer he started to stroll forward. Towards the woman he wanted to meet—the woman who was, although as yet she absolutely no idea of it, going to become his next mistress...

Kassia felt sweat trickling down her back and between her breasts. Her tee shirt was damp with it, and her cotton trousers grimed with dirt from where she'd been digging. She studied what she'd just unearthed—definitely a piece of a stirrup jar, once used for storing olive oil, over three millennia ago—then carried it carefully across to the table for initial cataloguing and identification.

'Ah, Kassia—what have you got there, hmm?'

The voice of the director of the excavation made her look up as she approached the table.

She opened her mouth to speak, to tell him what she'd found, but no words came. Her eyes had gone, as if pulled by a magnet stronger than that at the earth's core, to the man beside Dr Michaelis. He was completely out of place in his pale grey expensive business suit—top dollar, she could see at a glance—with his dark burgundy silk tie, high-gloss black shoes and gleaming gold watch around his wrist. He looked as though he'd just walked out of a board meeting.

But that wasn't what was making her stare. It was the

fact that this man, whoever he was—tall, lean and impeccably groomed—was, quite simply, the most incredible-looking man she had ever seen in her life...

Damos put a smile on his face. Just the right amount of a smile. But behind the nicely calculated smile his thoughts were racing.

So, this was Andrakis's daughter. Well, anyone looking less like the kind of woman he usually consorted with he could not envisage—she was the very opposite of glamorous. But he made the necessary allowances. She'd been kneeling in the dirt, in the heat, so he could hardly be surprised at her flushed face, the smudge of dusty soil on one cheek, and the hair liberally sprinkled with dust too, working its way loose untidily from the tight knot clamped at the back of her head. As for what she was wearing...

Damos's cataloguing was thorough—and ruthless.

A sweated-out shapeless tee in a singularly unlovely shade of mustard, and baggy cotton trousers with dirt on the knees in mud-brown. Feet stuck into worn trainers, also covered in dust and dried soil. Figure tall and gangly—impossible to tell more under those shapeless clothes, and quite probably that was just as well.

No. Kassia Andrakis, standing there, flushed and awkward, looking grubby and messy in her drab and dusty work clothes, with her shoulders stooped from kneeling, did not present an alluring image.

Can I really go through with this? Have an affair with this unlikely woman?

The question was in his head before he could stop it. Then his mouth tightened. His personal opinions of her as a female were irrelevant. She was a means to an end—that was all. And in pursuit of that end—which was lucrative and therefore a worthwhile one to him—he was prepared to put himself out.

As he was already doing.

He put a questioning expression on his face now. 'Will you show us?' he invited.

For a moment the woman he'd bestowed his smile upon did not move. She'd already frozen when she'd looked up from the shard cradled in her hands to see him standing there, beside the excavation's director, and now he could see she looked like a rabbit caught in headlights. Just before it was turned into mush on the road…

Well, maybe that was a promising sign, at least. Not that it surprised him. Without vanity, life had taught him ever since his teens that women liked what they saw when they looked at him. Even before he'd made his money that had been so. Now, with money made, the problem was more to keep them at arm's length. Though of course he enjoyed making his selection of those whose company he decided was most useful to him—and most pleasurable.

As 'new money'—very new indeed—he knew it did him no harm to be seen with a well-known face on his arm, so he liked to select women already in the public eye, from actresses and TV personalities to models and social-ites. All beautiful, all glamorous, all alluring. All of whom loved basking in the limelight and knew just how to do it. Women who knew, too, that being seen with him was good for them—their egos as well as their careers. No woman ever objected to an affair with him.

His eyes rested unreadably on this woman who—however

unlike any of her predecessors she looked, and the very an-
tithesis of glamour—was going to be next in that line. She
would not object either—he would make sure of it. She would
enjoy being his mistress.

But first he had to get her there…

She still had that rabbit-caught-in-the-headlights blank
expression, and to it was now added a stain of hot colour
across her already flushed cheeks that Damos knew had
nothing to do with the baking heat of the day.

As if belatedly realising she could not just stand there
and stare at him, she gave a start. 'Er…' she said, as if
speaking coherently were utterly beyond her.

Her director came to her rescue. He peered forward at
the grimy shard. 'Let me see—a shoulder, definitely, and
judging by the curve the original would have been at least
twenty centimetres tall. Did you see the rest of it?'

Damos saw Kassia Andrakis's eyes switch to her director, but it was as if it were an effort—as if there were
weights on them.

'Um… I think so—well, definitely more fragments. A
bit of the pouring lip and some of one of the handles.'

Her voice was distracted, and that high colour was still
in her cheeks.

It didn't suit her.

Damos flicked his eyes away, back to what they were
supposed to be looking at.

'Is that some kind of decoration I can make out?' he
asked, as if he were interested.

'Yes,' enthused Dr Michaelis.

He started to wax lyrical about the kind of ceramic decoration prevalent at the time, and Damos listened politely until the director ran out of things to talk about.

Damos turned his attention back to Yorgos Andrakis's daughter. 'So, can you show me how you go about getting the rest of the pieces out? I take it you have to go carefully?'

He saw her swallow, clearly still ill at ease.

'Um…' she said, then glanced uncertainly at her director.

He took charge immediately. 'I'll get this piece photographed and listed,' he said, deftly removing the shard from her hands. 'You show our visitor how we work.'

He seemed keen that she should do so, and Damos knew why. He was a prospective sponsor—whatever he wanted would be immediately offered.

Damos saw the colour deepen in Kassia Andrakis's face.

'Er…' she said, visibly hesitating again.

Her vocabulary was not large, it seemed, so Damos helped her out.

He took her elbow. 'Do show me,' he said. 'It's all quite fascinating.'

A look came his way—not one he expected. At first he took it for surprise—and then something more suspicious. He countered it by bestowing upon her a smile—a bland one.

'I've never visited an archaeological excavation before,' he said smoothly.

She stepped away slightly, so he had to let go her elbow.

'Why are you here now?' she posed.

There was something new about her—something… guarded. He didn't want it there. He wanted her open to him. Susceptible.

'I might be interested in sponsoring one,' he remarked, starting to head towards the trench she'd been working at.

'Why?'

Her question followed him. He looked back casually.

'It's tax deductible,' he said.

Her expression changed again. Tightened. If she was going to say something he wouldn't let her.

'Why disapprove? Wouldn't you rather excess profits from business were used to do something for the country—the community?'

He stepped carefully down into the shallow trench, mindful of his handmade shoes and his bespoke suit.

'OK, so show me what you do.'

He was aware of heads turning to see what was happening—aware, too, that he was getting attention from another female, a full-figured blonde. But he simply smiled blandly again, then hunkered down next to Kassia Andrakis.

'Mind your shoes,' he heard her say sharply. 'The dust gets everywhere.'

'Thank you for the warning,' he murmured.

He picked up her discarded trowel and held it out to her pointedly. She took it, but he sensed her reluctance.

'I really don't know why you're interested…' she said, resuming her kneeling. Her voice wasn't as sharp now, but it was still not exactly enthusiastic. 'You don't need to know or see the nitty-gritty to sponsor a dig. No need to get your hands dirty,' she said, and her voice had tightened again.

He got a look from her. One that told him, plain as day, that being hunkered down in a shallow trench, on a dusty dig on a remote island, in no way matched with a man wearing a ten-thousand-euro suit and five-thousand-euro hand-made leather shoes.

He met her look straight on.

'My hands have been dirty in my time, believe me,' he said.

He hadn't intended that edge to be in his voice, but he heard it all the same. And there was an edge inside him too. That this daughter of one of Greece's richest men, born herself into wealth, however much she was slumming it now, should presume to criticise him as she was so obviously doing...

She dropped her eyes, fixed her grip on the trowel. She pointed the tip at an uneven piece of undug earth.

'There's likely to be something under there,' she said. 'But you have to be very careful. Like this.'

She gently teased at the hard, dry ground with the tip of the trowel, picking up a nearby bristle brush with her other hand, and whisking away the loosened baked soil. As she did, Damos could see the convex curve of pottery revealed.

'This,' said Kassia Andrakis, 'is the first time sunlight has been on this piece of ceramic for over three thousand years.'

There was something in her voice—something that made Damos look at her. He wondered what it was, and then realised. It was a word he'd never spoken—but he knew what it was.

Reverence.

She was looking down at the humble piece of pottery as if it were a holy icon.

'Three thousand years,' she said again, and that same reverence was still there in her voice. 'Think of it—think of that age…so long gone. A world as vibrant as our own, with international trade routes, art and civilisation, learning and discovery…'

She looked across at him. It was the first time, Damos realised, she had actually made eye contact with him. He also realised the unflattering rush of colour to her cheeks was gone, and that her eyes were grey-blue, with almost a silvery sheen.

She gestured across the site with her trowel and went on, her voice not so much reverent now as impassioned. 'This place—all of it—is just a minute fraction of that world. A world that came to a catastrophic end three thousand years ago. So much is lost from that time—which is why we *must* do what we can to preserve what is left.'

Damos frowned. 'Catastrophic?' he echoed. He felt his interest piqued, which surprised him.

She nodded. 'Yes, the collapse of the Bronze Age all over the Eastern Mediterranean happened very suddenly. The population crashed…sites were abandoned. Living standards plummeted. It was a dark age—a very dark age.'

He got to his feet. 'Tell me more,' he said. 'Tonight. Over dinner.'

He didn't wait for her reaction, simply climbing out of the trench and walking towards Dr Michaelis, who was over by one of the tables. Dr Michaelis looked at Damos hopefully.

'Fascinating,' Damos said. He paused a fraction. 'So much so,' he went on, keeping his voice smooth, 'that I'd like to ask your young colleague—' he nodded back towards the trench '—to expound further. This evening. Over dinner.'

Dr Michaelis opened his mouth, then closed it again. Then a shrewd look—surprisingly shrewd, given his ingenuous enthusiasm previously—entered his eye. It was, Damos could see—and knew perfectly well why—tinged with surprise.

Not at the invitation.

At the person invited.

If it had been the voluptuous blonde he wouldn't have been so surprised.

Damos decided it was time to deflect both surprise and speculation.

'I know Kassia's father,' he said, giving a slight smile. 'He mentioned to me that I might encounter her here on this latest dig she's involved in.'

It was a lie, but that was irrelevant. And anyway, he did know Yorgos Andrakis slightly—they moved, after all, in the same affluent plutocratic circles in Athens.

Dr Michaelis's expression cleared. This was a suitable explanation for what his wealthy visitor and hopefully prospective sponsor had just put to him.

'Ah, of course,' he said genially. 'Now,' he said, 'is there anything else that I can tell you, or show you, that might be of interest to you? You have only to say!'

Damos smiled politely. 'Thank you, but what I have already seen is very impressive. I shall give your worthy endeavours very serious consideration. I am glad I had this opportunity to call by. I'm en route to Istanbul, on business, and this was a timely deviation.'

He held out his hand, let Dr Michaelis shake it in farewell, and turned to go. As he neared the cordoned-off perimeter he glanced back. Kassia's voluptuous blonde colleague, he noticed, not with any surprise, was covertly watching him. Kassia Andrakis, he saw, was not. Her attention was focussed right back on digging. Not on him at all.

A glint showed in the depths of his eyes. Kassia Andrakis might be ignoring him now—but for all that there was only one place she was going to end up.

His bed.

It was just a question of getting her there…

Pleased with his progress on that front so far, he headed back to his waiting car, parked on the dry, dusty lane leading through the overgrown olive grove beyond the dig. He got in, glad of the air con. Then, sitting back, he reached inside his jacket pocket, took out his gold monogrammed pen and a silver, monogrammed case, withdrawing a business card from it. After casually scrawling what he wanted to say on the back of it he handed it to his driver.

'Take this down to the female in that first trench. Not the blonde—the one with the mustard-coloured tee shirt.'

He sat back, eyes half closed, contemplating the next step in his campaign of eventual seduction. Dinner on his yacht would be the first step. And then… Well, he would have to see what would serve him best. A lot of money was riding on it—for himself.

As for Kassia Andrakis… She would enjoy her affair with him—women always did and she would be no exception. Why should she be? He would ensure her time with him was pleasurable, and she would enjoy his attentions.

She does not look like she's used to much male attention…

He felt himself frown slightly. There was something… troubling…about Kassia Andrakis. In the normal course of events she was not the type of woman he'd pursue—academic and studious, instead of glamorous and publicity-hungry. But because of his ambition to thwart her father's plans for her to his own advantage his focus of necessity must be on her.

His frown deepened. Yes, he had to make allowances for the fact that she'd been working all day long in the heat and the dust, so would hardly have been looking her best… There was a questioning look in his half-closed eyes now. And yet she seemed to be almost…self-effacing. Was that the word? About herself and her appearance. Flustered at even the most innocuous of attentions from him. She was tall, and yet her shoulders were hunched—maybe not just from kneeling, but as if she were trying to hide her height. And her straggly, tugged-back hair, covered in dust and needing a good wash, did absolutely nothing for her either.

It was as if she could not care less. Her awkward manner had been obvious. His expression changed suddenly. Until she'd made that impassioned plea for preserving the antiquities she was excavating. Then her eyes had lit, making him notice them for the first time…

Grey-blue, with that silvery sheen…

He frowned very slightly.

Intriguing—and quite at odds with the rest of her…

His ruminations about Yorgos Andrakis's daughter were interrupted by his driver returning, getting back into his seat, gunning the engine, driving off.

Damos put Kassia Andrakis and his plans for her out of his head, and took out his phone to check his messages.

CHAPTER TWO

Kassia sat on the bed in her little room in the *pension* she and others in the excavation team were staying at. She was staring at the back of the business card that had been handed to her by a chauffeur in a peaked cap that afternoon. A chauffeur of any kind—let alone in a peaked cap—was, to put it mildly, out of place on an island like this. But then the man who'd had the card delivered to her was totally out of place.

His handmade suit and shoes...his silk tie, gold watch—the whole caboodle!

But now at least she knew who he was.

Damos Kallinikos.

The name on the business card meant nothing to her, even though Dr Michaelis had told her he'd said he knew her father—hence inviting her, rather than him, the dig's director, for dinner this evening. Or that was what both Kassia and her boss could only assume, for there was certainly no other reason for singling her out. She wasn't the type of female who got asked to dine by drop-dead gorgeous men for her own sake—she knew that well enough.

As for the company Damos Kallinikos headed, according to the printed side of the business card, she'd never heard of that either. New money, by the sound of it. New money springing up in Greece after the financial crash in the first decade of the century, which had ruined countless lives and provided an opportunity for those canny and ruthless enough to take advantage to scoop up some bankrupt bargains.

It was what her father had done, she knew—boosting his already considerable wealth by snapping up businesses that had gone under in the crisis at rock-bottom prices. And he'd scooped up another round only a few years ago, when the global pandemic had hit, all but destroying Greece's vital tourist industry during those lengthy lockdowns that had immobilised the world, sending yet more businesses struggling. From deserted hotels to abandoned, unsellable, untransportable inventory, he'd turned their loss into yet more profit for himself.

Was that what this Damos Kallinikos had done too? Even if he hadn't, she could still hear his voice saying *'tax deductible'* as if in justification for caring about his country's treasured past. But she could hear Dr Michaelis's hopeful voice as well.

'Kassia, I do hope you will accept his dinner invitation and do your best to persuade him to sponsor us, so we can have a second season next year. Chatting to this man over dinner may well just swing it for us.'

She gave a sigh. Well, she would do her best—though she wasn't comfortable about it. Oh, not about pitching for sponsorship, but for a quite different reason.

As she sat on her bed Damos Kallinikos was vivid in her mind's eye—and so were his drop-dead good looks. Looks that had sent the colour flaring into her cheeks.

She made a face. What on earth did it matter that Damos Kallinikos looked the way he did? A man like that would not look twice at a woman like herself—someone totally lacking the kind of appeal that females like Maia, for example, possessed. Her mouth twisted. Hadn't her father drummed that into her all her life?

The sneering echo of her father's voice stung in her memory.

'Look at you! You're like a piece of string! A stick! Not even a decent face to take a man's eye off your stringy body! Your mother might have cost me a fortune to be rid of her, but at least she had looks!'

She sighed inwardly, accepting the truth of her father's criticism. Her mother was petite and shapely, with china-blue eyes set in a heart-shaped face and softly waving blonde hair. Kassia's own lack of looks were a constant cause for complaint by her father.

'No man will ever want you for yourself! It will only be for my money—for who I am, not you!'

That was his regular accusatory refrain.

She silenced the sneering voice. She was never going to let herself get sucked into her father's scheming, and to that end she should be grateful that her plain looks ruled her out of it. Had she looked like Maia, her father would be touting her all over Athens and beyond. Marrying her off to whoever would be most valuable to him as a son-in-law, making use of her to his own advantage.

As it was, thankfully, he'd all but written Kassia off, telling her to busy herself with her digging in the dirt and to keep out of his way, except for on those few unexpected occasions when he summoned her back to Athens for some social event where he wanted a daughter—even one as un-prepossessing as she was—at his side for some reason. She always obeyed such summons, for she knew her father had got himself made a patron of the provincial museum she worked for, and would make difficulties if she refused.

She stared down at the business card in her hand. This was another summons. In black scrawl on the back Damos Kallinikos had simply written:

The marina, eight o'clock.

She gave a sigh, wishing it were Maia who was being summoned—the girl had already expressed her envy at Kassia getting to spend the evening with the drop-dead fabulous Damos Kallinikos…

Impatiently she got to her feet, heading for the shower. Time to get on with getting ready for the evening ahead. Best not to think about it. Even more, best not to think about Damos Kallinikos—let alone his drop-dead fabulous looks. They were nothing to do with her, and she was the last person he'd ever be interested in in that way.

Yes, definitely best not think about him…

Damos glanced at his watch. It was just gone eight. He was standing on the foredeck of his yacht. Behind him a table had been laid for two. The yacht was moored at the far end of the marina to afford him more privacy. Privacy in which to start the process of seducing Kassia Andrakis.

How would she present herself this evening? Though she was no couture-clad socialite, as Yorgos Andrakis's daughter she would obviously know how to dress the part for an evening on a private yacht. So would she have done her best to glam herself up, or not? He had a gut feeling it would be 'not'. And a few minutes later, when he saw her appear in the marina, he knew he was right.

As she approached the foot of the quay he saw she'd changed out of her work clothes. But only, it seemed, to put on a fresh pair of wide-legged trousers—cotton and dark blue, cheap from a chain store—and a loose-fitting cotton top in a slightly paler blue. The worn, dust-covered trainers had been changed for flat canvas slip-ons. Her hair was brushed, and not straggly now, but still confined into an unflattering tight knot at the back of her head. Not a scrap of make-up adorned her face. She looked clean, neat and tidy—but that was about it.

He gave a mental shrug. He was not put out by her lack of effort to dress for dinner with him on his private yacht. After all, so far as she was concerned this evening was merely an extension of her work, nothing more. Yet even so...

Is there any other reason she makes so little effort with her appearance?

Damon's gaze narrowed slightly. Few women didn't care about their appearance in some respect. So why didn't Kassia Andrakis? Perhaps, though, the clue was in her surname. Had she been a high-profile beauty Yorgos Andrakis would doubtless have made use of it—so maybe she just preferred to keep a low profile?

His mouth thinned. Low profile or not, dressing down or not, Yorgos Andrakis was nevertheless ruthlessly planning to make use of her for his own ends.

As are you, yourself...

He silenced the thought. Yes, seducing Kassia Andrakis was in his interests, but nothing would happen that she did not want. And he reminded himself again that he would make sure she enjoyed their affair. Yet a flicker of something he could not name hovered a moment. He dismissed it. She was coming up to the yacht's mooring, looking up to where he stood by the prow.

'The harbour master told me this was yours,' she announced.

Damos smiled in a welcoming fashion. 'Indeed, it is. Come on aboard.'

He indicated the gangplank, a little way down the length of the yacht, and she went to it, stepping up to the deck, glancing around as she did.

'She's a new acquisition,' he said blandly.

'Very nice,' said Kassia Andrakis politely.

'Thank you. Not to be compared with your father's, of course.'

That got a reaction.

Her expression tightened. 'His is a ridiculous monstrosity!'

'A trophy yacht?' Damos nodded. 'But the helipad must certainly come in useful for speedy arrivals and departures, should the occasion arise. However, each to his own, and I prefer something a little more modest.'

Kassia's expression stayed tight. '*Modest* is relative,' she remarked. 'All yachts are trophy yachts.'

'Rich men's toys? I agree.' He smiled, refusing to take offence. 'Now, come and have a drink on this particular rich man's new toy.'

He indicated the foredeck, where one of his crew was waiting to serve drinks. Kassia moved forward, looking about her. She seemed tense, and Damos wanted to put her at ease.

'What may I offer you?' he asked politely. 'Champagne is often *de rigueur* on yachts—however modest! But perhaps you would prefer something else?'

'An orange juice spritzer, if that is possible,' came the answer.

'Of course.'

Damos nodded at the crew member, who disappeared below deck, to reappear shortly with Kassia's drink in a tall glass, and his own martini. His crew knew what he drank at this hour of the day, and he murmured his thanks as he took his glass, handing Kassia's to her.

'We'll dine in fifteen minutes,' he instructed, and the crew member nodded and disappeared again.

Damos came and stood beside Kassia—but not too close—as she sipped at her spritzer and looked back across the marina. It was busy, but not full. A couple of upmarket restaurants were positioned to take advantage of the moored yachts, and were doing a healthy trade. The lights from the marina and from the vessels moored, as well as the green and red harbour lights, all danced on the water, and the tinkling sound of furled sails and masts moving in the light breeze, and the deeper sound of hulls tapping against the stone moorings, added to the atmosphere.

'There's nothing like a harbour,' Damos said, looking around, his tone relaxed, trying to encourage her to do likewise. 'It's a haven from the open sea, but also a portal to that sea—to the voyages beyond. A harbour is a place of promise and opportunity. Now and down all the long ages past—and ages yet to come.'

He saw her turn her head to look at him. He smiled down at her.

'Too fanciful for a hard-nosed businessman who only sees archaeology as a tax-deductible instrument for greater profit?'

She didn't answer, but he got the impression she was studying him. Covertly, yes, but she was making some kind of assessment. Not reaching a conclusion, though. Wariness radiated from her—as it had that afternoon.

He took a meditative sip of his martini, looking out to sea past the harbour wall with its ever-blinking green and red lights.

'So, what kind of seafaring did they get up to in the Bronze Age?' he asked.

After all, that was what this evening was supposed to be about—expanding his knowledge of her field, so as to decide whether to invest in the work.

'It was extensive,' she answered. 'Right across the Mediterranean. Trade was widespread. As you probably know, the copper for bronze is plentiful in this region—Cyprus, of course, is named after the metal itself—but the tin needed to make bronze had to come from further afield.'

Damos could tell from her voice that she was somewhat stilted, and he focussed on drawing her out. Sticking to the subject she was most interested in—the one she believed he'd invited her here to discuss—he asked another question.

'How did they navigate in those days?' he posed.

'It's not my speciality,' came the answer, 'but if you're genuinely interested I can point you towards those who have made it theirs.'

There was sufficient inflection in her voice for Damos to know that she personally doubted that.

'In general, the Mycenaeans—and the Minoans and all the East Mediterranean peoples of the time—knew nothing of the compass, so they steered by the sun and the stars, and by the known distance from the shore plus speed and heading.'

'Dead reckoning?' put in Damos. 'As ever, right up until the eighteenth century, determining latitude was not so much a problem compared with determining longitude. That took highly accurate time-keeping—not available to the ancients. What was boat-building like in those times?'

'Boats were round-hulled, with square sail and oars which would one day develop into the famous biremes and triremes of the later Classical period—the battle of Salamis and so on. Sails, I believe, were considerably more limited than in later times.'

'Yes, it needed the development of the lateen sail—triangular in shape, but more difficult to operate—to allow vessels to sail much closer to the wind,' commented Damos.

She looked at him, clearly curious now. 'You know a lot.'

Damos gave a slightly crooked smile. 'I grew up in Piraeus and went off to sea as soon as I could. Working on merchant ships and crewing on the trophy yachts you so despise. It was the latter experience,' he said pointedly, 'that inspired me to be rich enough one day to buy my own yacht.'

'And now you do,' she said dryly, sipping at her spritzer.

He shook his head. 'No,' he said.

'No?' Kassia looked at him again. 'Is this only chartered?'

'No—as in, no, I don't only own my yacht—or charter it. I own a fleet—both leisure and merchant marine.'

'Oh,' she said. 'That's your money, is it?'

He smiled. 'Some of it.' He nodded along the line of the marina with its moored yachts. 'At least two of those are mine—chartered. Of course, like your father, my business interests are diverse. Ah!' He changed his voice, turning his head. 'Dinner arrives,' he said.

He held out one of the two chairs set at the table and Kassia sat down before he took his place as well. He exchanged some pleasantries with his crew members, who set down the dishes, placed a wine bottle in the chiller on the table, and discreetly retired.

'Do you eat seafood?' he enquired politely. 'If not, there is a vegetarian alternative.'

'No, that's fine,' came the answer.

She started to help herself from the central platter, piled high with prawns, calamari and shellfish, and Damos did likewise, adding leaves and salads to his plate, as did she. She didn't pick at her food, he noticed. So many of the females he consorted with visibly calorie-counted. Kassia Andrakis didn't look as though she did—or had any reason to. Despite her loose-fitting clothes, he could see she was definitely slender, not fulsome in her figure.

He eyed her through half-lidded eyes. She might be downplaying her appearance, but her slenderness was appealing, and now that he had more leisure to peruse her across the table, he could see that her face—still without make-up, but no longer flushed and dabbed with dusty soil—was fine-boned. Was that the English side of her? he wondered.

He found himself wanting to see if he'd just imagined that silvery sheen in her eyes when she'd enthused about her work. His half-lidded eyes moved their focus, and he also found that he wanted to know what she might look like with her hair loosed from its confining, studious knot.

What she might look like without any clothes at all…

His veiled gaze rested on her a moment longer. Had she obviously dressed herself up to the nines, glammed herself up for him, he might well have ventured, over a leisurely dinner and increasingly intimate conversation, to speculate that the night might end with her going down to his state-room to spend the night with him.

A woman who was interested in him that way, and in whom he had made clear a similar interest from himself, would have given signs of it—indicated that she found his attentions of that nature welcome to her and invited more of them. Until a mutual understanding of their respective willingness to take things further had been arrived at.

Kassia Andrakis, dressed down and unadorned, was showing no sign at all that she expected dinner with him to be anything other than what it purported to be. True, she was no longer flustered and awkward, as she'd been at the dig, but nor was she showing any visible awareness of him as anything other than a potential sponsor. No sign at all that she found him attractive as a man.

Should he be put off by that? He dismissed it out of hand. However composed she was being now, her initial reaction to him at the dig had been sufficiently revealing to him— he had no need to doubt it. But right now he wasn't even trying to get her to see him in that way. Coming on strong to her at this stage would be crass.

Worse, it might arouse her suspicions.

Because there was one thing he was discovering about Kassia Andrakis and he was clearly going to have to take it into account. She was no idiot. Oh, not just because she was a professional archaeologist, who obviously knew her stuff inside out, but because right from the start he had seen that she was perfectly prepared to assess, judge and downright challenge him on his apparent interest in her field and his declared intention of considering sponsoring it.

Disarming her wariness—and the assessing acuity she directed at him—was going to take some finessing.

His veiled gaze rested on her a moment.

He'd known from the start that Kassia Andrakis was nothing like the women he usually consorted with—and not just because the only reason for his own interest in her was her father's business plan and his own plans to thwart Yorgos Andrakis by the method he'd selected. No, Kassia Andrakis was different from his usual type of female in *herself*, not just in the circumstances of who she was and why. And therefore she had his attention—more so, he was finding, than he'd originally assumed.

Seducing her, he was starting to realise, was not going to be a simple case of showering flattering compliments upon her. She was a woman unused to receiving them and he was a man whose sexual interests were usually blatantly targeted at glamorously beautiful females. No, a far more subtle approach was going to be needed to disarm her— charm her into his bed.

A disquieting glint showed in the depths of his veiled gaze.

It will be a challenge...

The glint in his eyes deepened. And challenges were something he always found satisfying to achieve.

After all, his whole life had been a challenge. He had challenged the poverty into which he'd been born, changing it through determination, ambition and a hell of a lot of dogged hard work into riches.

So, he mused consideringly, keeping his speculative gaze on her as she ate, maybe Kassia Andrakis was not his usual type of woman, and maybe she was dowdy and unglamorous, and maybe her calm composure was showing no sign at all of responding to his masculinity, but for all that there might be something more enjoyable about seducing her than simply getting the result he was set on.

His thoughts coalesced. It might even be enjoyable for itself…as a challenge he would relish.

He was looking forward to taking it on.

Quite definitely…

That glint was back in his eyes, and he felt a sense of enticing anticipation…

Kassia was just beginning to feel her edge of acute wariness dissipating. Maybe she was getting used to Damos Kallinikos. He was being polite and making conversation, continuing to tell her about his time crewing on rich men's yachts.

'In some respects it was tougher than working on merchant ships,' he said dryly. 'Because you were on call twenty-four-seven, and rich men can be very demanding employers.'

She nodded, making a face as she did. Her father was inconsiderate of anyone who worked for him, and he would never dream of thanking them or showing any appreciation of their work and efforts.

She let her eyes rest on Damos Kallinikos for a moment across the table. She'd already noticed that he said please and thank you to his crew members, and passed the time of day with them pleasantly. That was to his credit, surely?

Her eyes flicked away again. She was conscious that she was not looking at him very much, or for very long—and she knew exactly why. Even though he was not, of course, focussing any kind of masculine attention on her—that was par for the course with her and men—that did not stop him being ludicrously good-looking. Whatever it was that made a man attractive, Damos Kallinikos had it in spades—and then some.

And then some more—

She dragged her thoughts away. No point assessing him in that respect. No point thinking how lethally attractive he was to her sex, with the way his dark hair feathered across his brow and his long eyelashes dipped down over those wine-dark eyes, or how his mouth curved into a half-smile that was tinged with a caustic humour as he regaled her with a particularly capricious demand by a yacht owner.

Their main course was being presented to them— chicken fillets in a wine sauce with saffron rice—and she got stuck in. Absently she lifted the wine glass that Damos Kallinikos had filled, and took a mouthful.

'What do you make of it?' he asked her.

'It's very good,' she said politely—because it was. 'Not that I know much about wine,' she went on. 'What is it?'

'A viognier varietal,' came the answer. 'One of my vine-yards has been experimenting...developing a vine that grows well on the volcanic soil here in the Aegean. I'm glad you like it.'

Kassia glanced at him. '*One* of your vineyards?'

'Yes—wine is one of the sectors that I can invest in with pleasure as well as profit in mind. And I have a particular interest in developing domestic wines. Greek wine should be better known internationally.'

'The blight of retsina?' Kassia rejoined dryly.

'Indeed—though retsina has its place. As do, of course, wines produced locally, entirely for local, low-cost consumption.'

Kassia gave a wry smile. Faint, but definitely a smile— her first of the evening, she realised with a little start.

'On excavations we don't run to more than the local table wines and beer of an evening.'

He looked at her, and she could see curiosity in his expression.

'How do you manage the adaptation?' he asked. 'You are Yorgos Andrakis's daughter—and yet you work digging up broken pots from the dirt.'

She paused a moment, then answered, choosing her words carefully.

'I don't spend much time in Athens—or in being Yorgos Andrakis's daughter. Besides,' she went on, 'I'm not always on excavations. Out of season I'm based at a provincial museum. I spend time studying our findings, cataloguing them, writing them up, contributing to papers, going to conferences—that sort of thing.'

'Not exactly a jet-set lifestyle,' Damos Kallinikos said mordantly.

She shook her head. 'Not my scene,' she agreed. She

looked across at him. 'And, since I have no head for business, the only thing for me to do as Yorgos Andrakis's daughter would be to go to parties and spend his money and be "ornamental". But…' she took a breath '…I am not "ornamental", so I'd rather do something useful and dig for broken pots in the dirt and catalogue them.'

He was looking at her now, and there was something in the way he was looking across the lamplit table that she found unnerving. She didn't know why. But it was unnerving, all the same. To stop it, she took a quick mouthful of her wine, and another mouthful of her tender and delicious chicken, and then quite deliberately moved the conversation on.

'Speaking of digging up broken pots—what was it that you wanted to know about our excavation?' she asked. 'Fire away with the questions—after all, it's what I'm here for.'

'So you are…' Damos Kallinikos murmured.

For just a moment that unnerving look was in his eye again—then it vanished. As if it had been cleared away decisively.

'OK, well, let me pick up on something you mentioned to me this afternoon,' he said. 'You said something about the collapse of Bronze Age Civilisation. I didn't know it had. Why did it—and when?'

Kassia felt herself relaxing—and engaging. This was familiar territory to her.

'The "when" is pretty well attested by the archaeological evidence—around 1200 BC or thereabouts. The "why" is more controversial and contentious.'

She reached for her wine again—it really was a very good wine after the table wines she was used to on digs.

'We can see that sites were being abandoned—the great palace complexes, like the most famous at Mycenae—and the population crashed. Linear B, the script of the Mycenaeans, all but disappears, and written Greek doesn't reappear until the adoption of the alphabet from the Phoenicians, in about the tenth century or so BC. The powerful Hittite empire in modern-day Turkey disappears too, and trade plummets in this post-Bronze Age period—though there is evidence of huge demographic changes, either from new arrivals, or from those economically displaced. It's the era of the still mysterious Sea Peoples, raiding and invading, and it's also the most likely time for the legendary Trojan War—'

She drew breath and plunged on, warming to her theme, running through the various possible causes of the collapse—from old theories about newly arriving Dorians from the north to current theories about climate change and the development of iron technology changing the balance of power and warfare. She was in full train, explaining the differences in smelting copper and tin to bronze, and the higher temperatures needed for smelting iron, when she stopped dead.

Damos Kallinikos had finished eating and was sitting back, wine glass in one hand, his other hand resting on the table. His eyes were half lidded, and she had the sudden acute feeling that she was boring him stupid.

She swallowed. 'I'm sorry. It's fascinating to me, but—'

He held up his hand. 'Don't apologise. I asked the question and you answered. I'm spellbound.'

For a moment she had the hideous feeling that he was being sarcastic. But then he leant forward.

'Your face comes alight when you talk with such passion,' he said.

His eyes met hers. Held hers.

Kassia couldn't move. Not a muscle.

Damos wanted to punch the air.

First contact.

First real him-to-her contact.

And all over the collapse of Bronze Age civilisation...

Well, so what? Whatever it took to bring her alive in the way it had just showed in her face was fine by him. Just fine.

Because, however it happens, I need to make personal contact with her—make the connection that can eventually lead to where I want it to go.

His eyes went on holding hers for a moment longer. As they did, he felt something go through him—something unexpected.

Was it the way her face had lit up and, yes, even in the soft light bathing them on the deck, the way that he'd caught that silvery glint in her eyes...?

It was doing something to him...

But it was time to back off—which was all part of the subtle approach that he knew was going to be necessary with her.

'You know,' he said, injecting just the right amount of humour and sincerity into his voice—both of which, he realised, he felt quite genuinely, 'if you intended to make a sales pitch for getting me to sponsor the dig, you've just made it.' He looked at her wryly. 'Doesn't it ever strike you that it is…unusual…to be so passionate about something that has not existed for over three thousand years?'

There was open curiosity in his voice. Kassia Andrakis was like no other woman he'd met, and the novelty of it was catching at him.

'I don't know,' she answered slowly. 'Maybe because it's a…a continuum. Like I said this afternoon, those people back then—however long ago it seems to us—were just like us. Living their lives as best they could. Just as we do.'

His wry look turned into a wry smile. 'That's not a bad way to live—then or now. Living our lives the best we can.' Damos heard his voice change. 'It certainly fuelled my determination not to stay poor—and to enjoy all that comes my way.'

He held her gaze for another moment. He put nothing into it of flirtation, nor any intimation of it. He wanted only to keep this moment of contact going. It was something to build on.

Then he glanced towards the wine chiller. 'Speaking of enjoying all that comes our way…this wine will go to waste if we don't finish it.'

He casually refilled her glass, and then his own, replacing the depleted bottle back in its chiller. He'd exaggerated the predicament of the wine—any leftovers would, he knew, be consumed below deck by the crew. One of the perks of the job, and something he was perfectly happy with.

He wanted to keep the atmosphere light, and so, taking another mouthful of his own wine, he sat back again.

'Does your work ever take you to Istanbul?' he asked casually. 'I'll be heading off there tomorrow.'

Kassia shook her head. 'I've visited Hissarlik—the site of Troy—in my time, but I have never made it to Istanbul.'

For a moment Damos considered inviting her to go with him, then set it aside. That would be premature. No, better just to use this evening as prep for planning his next encounter with her. Though where and how were yet to be decided on… One thing was definite, though. When he moved on in his seduction of her he did not want it to be in Greece, and certainly not in Athens. It needed to be kept private—very private. Until, with his goal in sight, it suited him for it to become very public knowledge…

Especially to Cosmo Palandrou.

There was a dark glint of anticipation in his eye. Because that would be the moment when he would have outmanoeuvred Yorgos Andrakis. Spiking his guns completely. Andrakis would have nothing to offer Cosmo—nothing that Cosmo would accept.

Damos's face hardened. No, Cosmo Palandrou would never want Yorgos Andrakis's daughter as his bride…

Not once he knows—and all of Athens knows!—that she's been my mistress…

Because for all that Cosmo might swallow Kassia being a dowdy archaeologist, not a glamorous trophy socialite, providing she brought with her the promise of the Andrakis riches, he wouldn't stomach marrying a blatant castoff of another man—and Damos Kallinikos at that. That would stick in his craw…would be an affront to his ego and self-esteem…and Andrakis's bid for his company would be dead in the water.

Leaving the way clear for me.

But he wasn't there yet. First he had to get Kassia Andrakis into his bed.

He brought his thoughts back to where they needed to be to achieve that end. How to build on where he'd got with her so far and take it to the next base.

'Do you travel much for your work?' he asked now, in a conversational manner.

'I go to conferences outside Greece sometimes. My mother lives in England, so a UK conference is a good opportunity to visit her.'

Damos paid attention—this was useful intel. He made a mental note to check out any likely UK-based conferences coming up on her subject that she might be likely to attend.

'Your parents are divorced, I take it…?' He trailed off, though he knew the answer perfectly well from his dossier on her.

'Yes, she's English and now remarried—unlike my father. Neither had any more children.' She made a face, half humorous. 'I don't think my mother wanted to ruin her figure, and my father didn't want to risk another hefty child maintenance divorce settlement!'

Damos knew that wry expression was back on his face.

'All rich men fear being married for their money. I've certainly become a lot more popular with women since I made money,' he heard himself saying, and wondered why he was saying it.

He frowned inwardly. Should he have said that? And why say anything about himself at all? This evening was about drawing Kassia out, exploring how best he could achieve his aims for her.

He saw she was looking at him now, but not unsympathetically.

'That's understandable,' she commented. 'Even I—if

you can believe it!—get attention paid to me simply because of my father!'

Damos relaxed. This was better—she was revealing
things about herself, not making him reveal things about
himself.

'Why "if you can believe it"?' He infused just the right
amount of uncomprehending curiosity into his voice.

He got a straight look and a straight answer. 'Why else
would they pay attention to me?'

She gave a short laugh, but it was without resentment. It
was infused, he thought, with wry resignation if anything.
And there was that air of indifference to her own appearance that he had picked up on from the start—as though it
was just not important to her.

There was a glint in her light eyes as she went on. 'Not
everyone, Mr Kallinikos, is sufficiently fascinated by
Bronze Age Civilisation as to want my company for dinner!'

This was approaching thin ice, he thought—time to
move the conversation off it. But gracefully...and perhaps
with some humour at his own expense to deflect the moment.

'Or as keen to find a good tax haven for this year's profits, don't forget!' he said lightly.

He got one of her wry half-smiles in return, and was
satisfied.

He returned to a subject he wanted to draw her out on.
Herself.

He found himself frowning inwardly for a moment. She
had been so upfront about not expecting men to be inter-

ested in her. Was that a good sign or a bad sign as far as his prospective seduction was concerned? It definitely meant he had to tread carefully, or her suspicions would be aroused.

Yet that was not his only reaction to her dispassionate disclosure. Surely it was sad that she wrote herself off the way she so obviously did?

No woman should do that.

His own voice cut short the thought. 'So, did you grow up in England?'

'Mostly, yes. I went to boarding school, and then university. I've always spoken Greek, though, and that's helped, of course, with my career.'

The crew were appearing, clearing away empty plates, replacing them with dessert.

'What can I tempt you with?' Damos invited.

He'd ordered a good range, from a sumptuous gateau St Honoré in towering choux pastry, to more frugal fruit and cheese.

Kassia made a face—she was definitely more relaxed with him, Damos could see, and he was highly satisfied with that. He was making good progress...

'It has to be the gateau,' she said. 'How can I possibly resist? But then I'll be virtuous and have some fruit afterwards.'

He laughed, cutting her a very generous portion of the towering dessert, spun with caramel and oozing cream, and then watching her start to tuck into it with relish and clear enjoyment.

It set a new thought running...

A woman who enjoys the sensuous pleasure of a rich dessert can enjoy other sensuous pleasures...

But that was a good way off yet. For now, it was just a question of continuing as he was doing—getting her to relax in his company, rounding off dinner with coffee, and then escorting her off the yacht to return her to her *pension* and her colleagues.

A good evening's work and a good base to build on. And time for him to consider his next move. And when he had he would act on it decisively, effectively. The way he always did in life.

She will be in my bed, and my plan will have succeeded.

It was a satisfying prospect.

He let his half-lidded contemplation of her sensuous enjoyment of the luxurious dessert linger a moment longer than it needed to, as into his head came again the thought that seducing Kassia Andrakis, so totally unlike any female of his considerable experience, and so completely oblivious of what he intended for her, would provide a distinct and novel challenge to pursue and achieve.

Not only because it would open the way to the lucrative business acquisition he wanted to make.

But for my own enjoyment...

A glint came into his veiled gaze. A glint of anticipation... and promise.

Yes, a satisfying prospect ahead indeed.

All that was required now was to plan his next move.

Kassia lay in her bed in her room but could not sleep. The evening she'd just spent kept playing inside her head. It shouldn't—but it did.

It shouldn't for one obvious reason. She'd had dinner with Damos Kallinikos solely to encourage him to sponsor the excavation—nothing else.

And yet it was hard—impossible—to put it out of her mind and go to sleep. Even though there was obviously no point in dwelling on it.

Because what would be the point of remembering how it had been to sit out on that foredeck with Damos Kallinikos, feeling the low swell of the sheltered harbour water beneath the hull, with the stars high above, the warmth of the night air, the scent of the flower arrangement on the table and the glint of light on the glasses filled with chilled white wine? And what would be the point of remembering talking with him, hearing the timbre of his voice, responding to his questions, feeling that half-lidded glance on her, knowing that if she let her own eyes settle on him they would simply want to gaze and gaze...?

No point at all. No point, she told herself sternly, in doing anything but reminding herself that a man with looks like his—looks that had reduced her to flustered silence when she'd first set eyes on him that afternoon at the dig—was way out of her league—stratospherically out of her league. Oh, he'd been polite, and civil, and he'd conversed easily with her. But she had to face it squarely on. A man like him was not going to think anything more of her beyond the reason he'd invited her to his yacht.

She'd been wary about going in the first place, but as the evening had progressed she'd relaxed more. The fact that he was so totally out of her league had made it easier, in a strange way. The kind of women he would take a personal interest in would be as fabulous-looking as he was…ritzy and glitzy and gorgeous.

Not like me.

For a second, fleeting and painful, she felt a sudden longing in her. Oh, she knew she was nothing much to look at, and she accepted that undeniable truth about herself—had even said it straight to Damos Kallinikos's face. And yet for a few searing moments protest rose in her.

Oh, to be possessed of the kind of full-on glamorous beauty that would make Damos Kallinikos look twice at her…

More than look at her…

She crushed the longing down. There was no point wishing for what was impossible. No point at all.

And no point replaying in her head the evening that had just passed.

Damos Kallinikos had briefly entered her life, and tomorrow he was sailing on to Istanbul.

And she would be going back to digging in a hot, dusty trench.

She'd done what Dr Michaelis had asked of her—made a successful pitch for sponsorship, as Damos Kallinikos himself had told her. All she could do was hope it was enough to make him follow through with it. As for the man himself—there was no reason for their paths to cross again.

None whatsoever.

So what he looked like, and what she looked like, and what she might long for or not long for, or even think about him, remembering the evening that had been and was now gone was, she told herself yet again, completely pointless.

With that final adjuration to herself, she turned on her side, closed her eyes, and determined to sleep.

CHAPTER THREE

DAMOS RELAXED BACK into his first-class airline seat. His mood was good. His generosity in making it known to Dr Michaelis that, yes, he would indeed sponsor next year's season, had been rewarded when, after he'd made a carefully casual enquiry after Kassia Andrakis, the excavation's director had told him she was currently in England, visiting her mother. Damos had noted with decided interest that she was going on to Oxford afterwards, for a conference.

It was exactly the intel Damos had wanted.

And now he, too, as it happened, was also headed for that very city...

It had been nearly three weeks since their dinner on his yacht, and he needed to make his next move. Yorgos Andrakis, so his information on that front was indicating, was definitely softening up Cosmo Palandrou, spending time with him and paying him attention.

For a moment Damos frowned. Yorgos Andrakis might want to marry his daughter off to Cosmo, but why would Kassia co-operate? After all, she had her own career, and she didn't seem interested in being a fashionable socialite, so why would she do what her father wanted and marry a man almost as repellent as her own father?

His frown deepened. Not many people stood up to Yorgos Andrakis—maybe he would simply bully and browbeat Kassia until giving in was easier than opposing him? In which case…

In which case, having an affair with me that puts Cosmo Palandrou off her totally will actually be to her benefit. As well as mine.

It was a reassuring thought.

The flight attendant pausing by his seat to enquire what he might like to drink distracted him. He glanced up at her. She was blonde, good-looking, and it was obvious to him that she liked what she was seeing too. He smiled, but it was a perfunctory smile only as he gave his order.

For now there was only one female who was the focus of his thoughts and his attentions.

Kassia Andrakis.

And it was time to get to second base with her.

Kassia gazed up at the plaster replica statue of the two-metre-high *kouros* looming over her in the Ashmolean Museum. She always liked to look in at the Ashmolean whenever she was in Oxford, and it was a pleasant way to while away the afternoon before the opening dinner of the conference that started on the morrow.

She was glad to be in England—not just for a conference, where her old professor would be giving a presentation, or because she'd spent a few days seeing her mother, but because it was a welcome change of scene for her.

For all her determination, putting that evening on Damos Kallinikos's yacht out of her head was proving more difficult than it should. Of course it was pointless to dwell on it—she kept telling herself that robustly—but for all that it would replay in her mind at odd moments, bringing it vividly into her thoughts again. Bringing *him* vividly into her thoughts again…

Which was ridiculous, as well as pointless. It was nearly three weeks ago, and Damos Kallinikos had been and gone from her life.

A voice behind her spoke.

'This must be my lucky day—the perfect person to expound to me on this monumental youth.'

Kassia froze. Disbelievingly, she turned. As if she had conjured him from her very thoughts, Damos Kallinikos was standing there.

'What on earth…?' she heard herself say. Incredulity was spearing in her—and also something quite different from incredulity…something that made her breath catch in her throat. 'What are you doing here?'

Damos Kallinikos smiled. 'The same as you, it seems. Admiring this very handsome chap.'

'But what are you doing in Oxford at all?'

There was still incomprehension in her voice, she knew. And incomprehension might be uppermost in her, but it was not her only reaction to what she was seeing. Her pulse had given a hectic kick, and not just from surprise. She felt suddenly breathless.

'Oh, I've got some business here,' he said, his voice casual. 'What about you?'

'A conference,' she said mechanically. 'It gets going this evening—at a pre-conference dinner—then runs tomorrow and the day after.'

She was still fighting down surprise—and that other,

completely irrelevant reaction to seeing him again. Fighting down the urge to just gaze at him…helplessly and gormlessly.

'More Bronze Age, I take it?' Damos Kallinikos was asking conversationally.

She nodded abstractedly. 'My old professor is giving a presentation on Mycenaean battle tactics.'

She got Damos Kallinikos's wry smile. 'Yet more I haven't a clue about,' he said. His glance went past her to the gigantic *kouros* behind her. 'Just like this guy. So, tell me about him. Why's he smiling like that?'

She turned sideways, between Damos and the *kouros*. 'Oh, that's the famous Archaic smile. It's on loads of statues from that era—between the Dark Ages that followed on from the collapse of the Bronze Age, to just before the Classical Era proper in the fifth century. Statuary in the Archaic period was very static—probably deriving from Egyptian styles. Just the left foot forward… Greek sculpture only really took off in the fifth century—'

She was gabbling, she knew she was, but shock—and so much more—was still overpowering her.

She felt her arm taken.

'Fascinating,' Damos Kallinikos murmured. 'So, what else has this place got? I only wandered in as I'm staying at the hotel opposite.' He guided her towards some display cabinets a little way off. 'What's this lot in here?' he asked.

Mechanically, Kassia started to expound upon and explain the contents, amplifying the descriptive cards. Her head was reeling. How had Damos Kallinikos suddenly turned up like this, out of the blue, in the Ashmolean Museum, of all places? How come he was here in Oxford on business at all, when she was here for a conference? And how come he just happened to be in the museum when she was?

Well, coincidences do happen, she thought helplessly. *However unlikely, sometimes you did just bump into someone you never expected to.*

He was still listening to what she was telling him, distracted though she knew she sounded, but when they'd exhausted two more display cabinets he held up a hand.

'That's it—you've hit the limit of my brain capacity! Time for tea.'

'Tea?' Kassia said blankly, as if he'd suggested something she'd never heard of.

'Yes, afternoon tea. My hotel does a very good one, so I'm told. Come along—you must be parched after that ancient history lesson you've given me.'

Once again she felt her arm taken, then she was being guided up the stairs to the entrance level, and out into the fresh late-summer air.

'That's my hotel,' Damos Kallinikos said, pointing across the road.

Kassia was not surprised—it was the most expensive in Oxford.

He guided her down the broad flight of shallow steps from the museum to the pavement, and then across the road. Kassia was still trying to make sense of what was happening… encountering Damos Kallinikos again, totally unexpectedly. And why he was bothering to spend time with her.

She tried to rationalise it in her head. Well, why shouldn't they have tea together? They did know each other, albeit slightly, and he had, after all—so she'd heard from Dr

Michaelis—agreed to sponsor next year's season. Maybe that explained his asking her more about the ancient world?

Yet as they settled down to be served it was not antiquities that Damos asked her about.

'Do you know Oxford well?' he posed.

'Not very well, no,' she answered. 'Only for conferences, really.'

'This isn't your old university?'

She gave a self-deprecating laugh. 'No, nothing so lofty! I went to a north-country uni—decidedly redbrick.'

He frowned. 'Redbrick?'

'Just about any university more modern than Oxbridge,' she explained dryly.

'Oxbridge?' He frowned again.

'Short for Oxford and Cambridge,' she expounded. 'One is either Oxbridge or one is not,' she went on, even more dryly. 'I'm definitely *not*. But I do get to go to conferences here sometimes.'

He looked at her. 'It sounds very elitist.'

She could hear an edge in his voice. Condemnation.

'All of academia is elitist, really, if you think about it. An ivory tower. It's a privilege to be part of it—even if I'm only from a humble redbrick or a provincial Greek museum. Speaking of which,' she went on, 'Dr Michaelis is delighted at your decision to help fund next season's dig.'

'Well, I hope he's thanked you for your sterling efforts to that end over dinner that evening!' came the reply.

'I didn't really do anything,' Kassia said awkwardly. 'Just bored on about the Bronze Age.'

'It was,' said Damos Kallinikos, 'far from boring.'

His eyes—dark, thickly lashed, and with an expression

in them that did things to her heart rate—were resting on her for a moment, and to her dismay Kassia felt her cheeks flush with colour. To her relief, the waiter arrived, setting down their repast. It was lavish in the extreme, with savouries, scones, jam and cream, and sweet pastries.

Kassia's eyes widened.

'I'll never manage the conference dinner tonight if I eat all this!' she exclaimed humorously.

'Looks good, doesn't it?' Damos agreed cheerfully. 'Get stuck in!'

Kassia did—it looked too good to resist. And then she realised the waiter was setting down not just a teapot, but two glasses of gently fizzing sparkling wine.

'To celebrate,' Damos said, handing her one and lifting his own.

'Um…celebrate what?' Kassia asked, confused.

He smiled across at her. 'Afternoon tea,' he said. 'One of the great contributions to civilised life!'

Kassia laughed—she couldn't help it. And nor could she help feeling her cheeks colour again, just because of the way Damos Kallinikos was smiling at her.

Oh, dear God, but he was just so…so…

Descriptive words failed her—and were quite unnecessary. Because the colour in her cheeks, and the skipping of her heart rate, the sense of effervescence in her veins, was telling her just how strongly she was reacting to seeing him again.

I thought our paths would never cross again. That he'd been and gone from my life. And now…

Now here she was, totally unexpectedly, totally out of the blue, having afternoon tea with him in Oxford's best hotel…

As coincidences went, running into him like this as she had, it was beyond amazing.

'Cheers!' said Damos Kallinikos, clinking his glass lightly against hers, smiling across at her with his warm, wonderful smile.

She took a sip of the sparkling wine, feeling suddenly light-headed, dipping her eyes. Whatever extraordinary coincidence had caused Damos Kallinikos to step back into her life, even if just for afternoon tea, she was very, very glad of it.

It was definitely worth enjoying.

Damos set down his glass and reached for one of the delicately cut sandwiches. Satisfaction was filling him. Kassia had accepted completely that there was nothing more behind their encounter than sheer coincidence, just as she'd accepted his invitation to afternoon tea.

She clearly welcomes meeting me again, and is happy to spend time with me.

Second base had definitely been achieved. Now it would be a question of building on it. OK, so for the next couple of days she'd be occupied at the conference, but after that…? Time to put himself in her diary.

'What will you be doing after the conference?' he asked. 'I think you mentioned over dinner that you visit your mother when you're in the UK…?'

Kassia reached for a savoury tart and started to eat it delicately. Damos surveyed her through half-lidded eyes. Though she was neatly dressed, the long-sleeved top and trousers she was wearing were very unexciting, he found himself thinking. She was still not wearing any make-up, and her hair, though again very neat, was simply pulled back into a knot on her nape.

Why does she not make more of herself?

His gaze rested on her assessingly. He had been prepared for her lack of chic, but he still wondered at her apparent complete lack of interest in fashion or her appearance. His gaze lingered for a moment. And yet her bone structure was good, and there were those light, almost silvery eyes, and her slender figure showed itself off in her delicately sculpted collarbones and the elegant length of her forearms.

Her reply to his question distracted his thoughts.

'I spent a few days with her before I came to Oxford,' she was saying. 'She lives in the Cotswolds, so not too far from here.'

'Very scenic, I believe, the Cotswolds,' Damos commented.

He knew more about her mother now—he'd had her checked out. She was remarried to a retired industrialist, enjoyed a plentiful social life, and holidayed a lot. Just how much communication she had with her ex-husband he wasn't sure, but he could not risk it. Could not risk word of his forthcoming affair with Yorgos Andrakis's daughter getting back to Athens.

Fortunately, his sources had indicated that she was likely to be taking off for an annual late-summer holiday at her husband's villa in Estepona, in southern Spain, so she should be off the scene shortly. That would fit in nicely with his own planned timing.

'I don't know much about this part of England,' he went on musingly. 'Apart from Oxford itself, and the Cotswolds, what else is worth seeing? I ask because I've business in

London late next week, so I've some days free for sight-seeing here. What do you recommend?'

'Um…it depends what you like,' Kassia replied.

She sounded awkward again.

'Oh, the usual tourist things,' he said airily. 'What about grand stately homes? England is famous for them, after all.'

'Well,' she ventured hesitantly, 'Blenheim Palace is only a few miles out of Oxford, if you want to stay local.'

'Sounds perfect,' he said, taking another savoury and starting to demolish it. 'Why don't you show it to me?'

'Me?' She looked taken aback.

'Yes, we could make a day of it—after your conference.'

'Er—um…' Her hesitation was palpable.

'Do you have something else planned?' he posed.

She might, for all he knew. Presumably she had friends in England. She might have arranged to see them while she was here, as well as her mother.

'No…no, not really,' she replied awkwardly. 'I might visit an old schoolfriend, but not till next weekend.'

Damos smiled encouragingly. 'Good,' he said, and started on the scones.

He was past second base and things were going just the way he wanted them to. He spread cream and jam generously on his cut scone, took a hearty bite, and with his free hand indicated the remaining delicacies.

'Eat up,' he said cheerfully. 'And tell me all you know about Blenheim Palace. Now that we'll be visiting it together…'

Kassia sat in her seat at the conference, but her mind was not on the presentation. It was back on having afternoon tea with Damos Kallinikos.

Damos Kallinikos, who had turned up out of the blue, in Oxford, taken her off to tea at his hotel, and then lined her up to visit Blenheim Palace with him the day after tomorrow.

Why?

That was the question in her head. Why did he want to spend more time with her? Accosting her at the Ashmolean might just be explicable, with reference to his decision to fund Dr Michaelis next season. But taking her to tea? Going off to Blenheim with her?

It didn't make sense.

I'm the last kind of female a man like him would spend time with.

She knew that for certain now. Back in Greece she'd been unable to resist the temptation of looking him up on the Internet—and what had leapt onto her screen had not been his business affairs, in which she was not really interested anyway, and besides he'd already told her it was marine and shipping and so on, but what interested the tabloids and celebrity magazines. And that was, quite definitely, his social life. A social life which always seemed to involve him having a beautiful female draped on his arm. She'd counted at least two women familiar from the TV, one of whom was a fashion model, and another two who were well-known socialites in Athens. What they all had in common was the fact that they were show-stoppingly beautiful and glamorous...

And if there was one description which would never be used of herself it was that.

Just as she had in her bedroom after that dinner on his yacht, she felt a wave of sudden longing go through her. Oh, to be capable of looking glamorous—beautiful—show-stopping—stunning!

But it was hopeless. She'd always known that.

Her father had spelt it out brutally, with his sneering criticism of her gangly frame, and even her mother, far more kindly, had sighed because nothing she ate ever seemed to give her any curves or stop her growing so tall. On top of that, her hair was mouse-coloured and hung limply if loosened, and her eyes were too pale, her lashes likewise. So she'd never bothered trying to dress fashionably, never bothered to do anything with her lank hair, never bothered to wear any make-up.

But then in the world she lived in none of that mattered. Academia might be an ivory tower, as she'd remarked to Damos the day before over tea, but in it you were never judged on your looks.

After all, she thought, it was not as if she never dated. She had as a student and still did—fellow archaeologists and academics—only it was never with anyone remotely in Damos Kallinikos's league.

She gave a sigh. She must stop thinking about him. Yes, it was unlikely that he wanted to spend a day visiting Blenheim with her, but maybe he just preferred to have some kind of company, and someone who was English and knew a fair amount about history in general. Anyway, she'd agreed, and that was that.

We'll spend the day there, see the palace, then he'll drop me back in Oxford and wave goodbye.

Paths diverging again.

And Damos Kallinikos would be out of her life, and she wouldn't see him again.

Again.

* * *

'Now, that,' Damos said, 'is impressive!'

He gazed at the huge bulk of Blenheim Palace, now revealed in all its massive glory after their walk from the
car park.

'It is,' Kassia agreed.

She still couldn't quite believe that Damos had followed
through on his casual suggestion that she accompany him
here—and yet here she was. He'd picked her up in a hire
car—a very swish one—from outside the college where
the conference attendees had been staying. She'd felt shy
at first, and awkward, as they'd headed out of Oxford, but
Damos had been relaxed, and clearly putting himself out
to put her at her ease.

In return, she would do her best to be a helpful guide
for the day, she told herself firmly.

'Didn't you tell me over tea the other day that it's the
only non-royal palace in England?' Damos asked her now,
as they strolled into the huge and impressive Great Court
in front of the grand entrance, along with the many other
visitors the palace attracted.

'Yes—though ironically it's sometimes used in films as
a substitute for Buckingham Palace!' she replied.

'Remind me why it's got a German name,' Damos said.

'It's named after the first Duke of Marlborough's most
famous victory, at the Battle of Blenheim, in Bavaria in
1704. England and Austria were fighting the Bavarians
and Louis XIV of France. It was designed by John Van-
brugh and took over ten years to build. It's so large that apparently the first Duchess, the infamous Sarah Churchill,
bossy confidante of poor Queen Anne, hated it. She com-

plained the kitchens were so far from the dining room the food was always cold!'

Damos laughed, turning his head to look at her. 'You know all this stuff without even consulting the guide book—it's amazing!'

She made a self-deprecating face. 'Well, I guess history overall is my subject, really—if you like one period you like lots. I've been here before, too, when I was a schoolgirl. Though not since.' She glanced sideways at him. 'It's good to come again—thank you for inviting me,' she said politely.

'Thank you for accepting my invitation,' he responded promptly.

There was a glint in his eye. She could see it.

'I can tell you not that many females of my acquaintance would think this a fun day out!'

She looked away. No, the kind of women he ran around with—those beautiful and glamorous TV personalities, models and socialites—wouldn't be seen dead playing tourist like this. Her thoughts flickered. It wasn't the kind of outing a man like him would be likely to enjoy either, she'd have thought. It didn't exactly compare with sailing around on his private yacht… *One* of his private yachts, she reminded herself tartly.

But maybe I'm just overthinking it. OK, he's rich now, but he wasn't born to it, so he probably doesn't think it beneath him to be a tourist. After all, I don't think it beneath me—and I was born to wealth.

Not that she lived that kind of life. She far preferred the low-profile existence she had—working as an archaeologist, having as little to do with her father as she could. Most of the time he let her alone, but from time to time he summoned her to Athens to play her role as his daughter, such as it was, and attend dinner parties, functions—that kind of thing. Her father made it clear to her on such occasions that she was not to put herself forward, but to be meek and docile, and not bore people with all her 'archaeology nonsense', as he called it.

'It's bad enough being saddled with a daughter as plain as you,' he would say dismissively.

She would have preferred not to be summoned, but was mindful that her father had made himself a patron of the museum she worked at—to defy him would be to lose that patronage, she knew. So, since he didn't often want her in Athens, going along with his demands didn't seem too onerous an obligation, although she was always glad when it was over. Her father was not pleasant company...

Of her two parents, she far preferred spending time with her mother—not that her butterfly of a mother, affectionate though she was, ever had much time for her in between her constant social engagements and flitting abroad on holidays with her husband. Kassia was fond of her mother, and indeed her stepfather, whose stolid patience was a good foil for his flighty wife, but she didn't see a great deal of them. It had been good, though, to spend a few days with them on this visit, before they'd headed out to Spain.

'OK, where are we going first?'

Damos's question interrupted her thoughts.

'Can you face a tour of the palace?' she asked. 'The state apartments are as impressive as the exterior.'

'Why not? Then we can explore the grounds afterwards.'

They made their way to where the tours began. Inside,

Damos gazed around the magnificent rooms appreciatively, and gave a low whistle.

'That first duke certainly made good for himself!' he murmured admiringly, pausing to take in all the splendour.

'He got to the top from relatively humble beginnings. He was very ambitious—as was his wife,' she commented dryly.

'There's nothing wrong with ambition.'

The acerbic note in Damos's voice was audible. Kassia looked at him.

'Without ambition, hard work gets you nowhere,' Damos said. 'With it, anything can be achieved.'

'I… I suppose it depends on what you want,' Kassia said cautiously.

She had a feeling she was hitting Damos Kallinikos on a nerve. Maybe one that was still raw, given his own rise from humble beginnings. He was looking at her with an expression in his eyes she hadn't seen before.

'You're second-generation wealth, Kassia,' he said. 'Oh, you may work diligently in your career, but you have that cushion of wealth behind you all the same. It gives you a sense of security, of expectation, that you are scarcely aware of.'

She swallowed. 'I know I've had a privileged upbringing, but I try not to exploit it.'

A short laugh came from him. She did not hear any humour in it. Only vehemence as he spoke, biting out the words.

'Privileged, all the same. You've never felt the hunger of an outsider. University was out of the question for me. You said to me at the dig—I remember it quite clearly—that

I wouldn't want to get my hands dirty. But I've done my
years of hard manual labour, believe me. While you were
enjoying the luxury of higher education, paid for by your
father, I'd been working since I was fifteen on the docks—
crewing on private yachts and merchant marine, working
to make money, save money, give myself a financial base
and make something of myself, haul myself up the ladder
rung by rung. It isn't easy starting from scratch. It takes
determination and, yes, ambition—and I've got both, or I
would never have achieved what I have.'

Kassia was silent. Her father, too, was ambitious and
determined—ruthlessly so. Seizing every and any opportunity to make money, boasting of how he'd built himself up
from nowhere by snapping up ailing businesses driven to
the wall during Greece's prolonged financial crisis fifteen
years earlier at rock-bottom prices. He'd done it again during the more recent pandemic. Then he'd sacked as many
employees as he could, stripped out any valuable assets,
and run the businesses at the least cost and greatest profit
to himself, before moving on to his next acquisition. He
was probably working on another one right now—he usually was.

'I apologise. I didn't mean to speak so critically.'

Damos's voice cut across her darkening thoughts, no
longer vehement now, and she was relieved. Surely there
was no reason to think Damos Kallinikos as ruthless as
her father? But then, where did the balance come between
ambition and ruthlessness?

'Please,' she responded immediately, 'I didn't mean
to condemn simply being ambitious, or wanting to make
money. It's just that my father…' She hesitated, then went

on awkwardly, 'Well, you must know his reputation for ruthlessness in business, riding roughshod over people, making use of anyone he can to achieve his ambitions—'

She broke off, not wanting to compare Damos to her father. Wanting to think better of him.

'Whatever your father's business practices are, Kassia,' Damos said tightly, '*I* made my money honestly.'

For a moment she met his eyes full-on, knowing there was a troubled look in her own. Then she looked away, blinking. She felt a brief touch on her arm. Damos was speaking again, his voice lighter now, but still pointed.

'Let's change the subject—not spoil this very pleasant day. So...' he took a breath, making his voice warmer '...what's this next room?'

He guided her forward into an adjoining chamber as magnificent as the last one. They were all magnificent—a breathtaking enfilade, with doorways ornamented, walls bedecked with tapestries and portraits, floors richly carpeted, curtains heavy and silken, furniture gilded and ornate, tables laden with silver and priceless porcelain.

'Not exactly homely,' Damos said dryly.

Good humour was back in his voice now, and Kassia was glad. Relieved. She made her tone of voice match his.

'Well, these are the state apartments, so they are designed for showing off grandeur and opulence! I'm sure the current Duke has a wing or whatever, for himself and his family that is far cosier,' Kassia replied.

'That's reassuring,' Damos observed. 'These massive rooms are OK in the summer, but everyone must freeze in a British winter!'

Kassia laughed. That moment of friction between them had been uncomfortable, but it was over. She could relax again.

'English country houses of the time were infamous for being freezing, however many fireplaces they had! I believe it wasn't until the impoverished aristocracy started marrying all those American dollar princesses at the end of the nineteenth century that things like central heating were installed.'

'Dollar princesses?' Damos posed.

'American heiresses to all the new money being made in the USA at the time. They arrived in Europe to snap up titled husbands in exchange for their huge dowries. Consuelo Vanderbilt was one. She married the Duke, the cousin of Winston Churchill, whose own mother, Jenny Jerome, was another dollar princess.'

'Tell me more,' said Damos, and Kassia did.

She was much happier talking about such things than touching on how Damos Kallinikos had made his money and hoping it wasn't anything like the way her father had made his. Her father was the most ruthless man she knew, stooping to any level to increase his wealth.

I don't want Damos to be like that—to be anything like him!

Why, she didn't want to question—except she knew that she wouldn't want anyone to be like her father.

And why should Damos be like him? There are plenty of decent ways of making money—hard work, high achievements. No need at all for him to be as ruthless as my father...

State apartments all viewed, as well as Winston Churchill's birth room—surprisingly modest, as Damos pointed out to her—they made their way outdoors. The warmth of the day wrapped around them, and Kassia felt her spirits warming too.

'Lunch?' suggested Damos.

Kassia nodded.

'Let's sit outside, and decide where to go next,' he went on, leading the way to one of the several eateries Blenheim offered—this one with outdoor seating in a courtyard leading to the gardens beyond.

They chatted amiably over a light but tasty lunch of soup and a sandwich for her, and traditional English sausages, mash and gravy for Damos, which he ate with relish. They rounded off the meal with coffee and a selection from the bakery.

'It's nice that you don't feel the need to calorie-count,' Damos said, and smiled as Kassia finished off her rich brownie.

She made a face. 'One of the perks of being a piece of string!' she said lightly.

'String?'

She gave a little shrug. 'It's what my father always calls me. A piece of string.'

Damos's eyes narrowed. 'Tell me,' he said, 'you're taller than he is, aren't you?'

Kassia looked surprised. 'Well, yes—but then I'm taller than a lot of men. You're one of the few exceptions—' She broke off, not wanting to be too personal. 'My mother, by contrast, is petite,' she went on. 'She always says—'

She broke off again.

'She always says…?' Damos prompted.

Kassia gave another shrug. 'She always says she

thought I'd never stop shooting up. That I must take after her grandfather.'

Into her head came her mother's familiar next words.

'Of course, for a man it doesn't matter, being so tall...'

Her mother would have loved her to be petite and curvaceous, as she herself was. To be pretty and ultra-feminine simply for Kassia's own sake. Her father, by contrast, had she been possessed of such beauty, would have doubtless touted her off in fashionable circles and probably tried to marry her off to someone he could make use of. Another businessman...a politician—it wouldn't have mattered who to her father, so long as the marriage benefited himself. Her own preference would have been irrelevant to him.

At least her lack of looks protected her from that kind of pressure. That was something to be grateful for, she thought ironically. Except that now...

She gave a silent sigh. A man like Damos Kallinikos was used to having only beautiful and glamorous women at his side, and she knew that for the first time in her life she would have loved to be in that league. She sighed again. She was yearning for something that was impossible... quite impossible.

She became aware that Damos was looking at her speculatively, with a look in his eyes she hadn't seen before. She wondered at it. But then it was gone.

He picked up his coffee cup, draining it. 'Time to hit the gardens,' he said. 'How about starting with the water terraces? They're the closest.'

'Sounds good.'

Kassia smiled. She was glad of the change of subject— talking about herself had made her feel self-conscious, and not in a good way. Exploring Blenheim's glorious gardens would be far more pleasant.

They made their way out of the courtyard and took the path leading to the upper water terrace, adjacent to the west front of the palace. It was certainly impressive, and they wandered leisurely along the paths around the ornate stone ponds. Kassia paused for a moment to trail her fingers in the cool water, and Damos did likewise, having turned back the cuffs of his shirt beforehand. Kassia tried not to let her gaze linger on the lean strength of his wrists, or the square solidity of his hands. Hands, she supposed must have hauled up sails and set rigging and done any amount of hard manual labour in their time.

Now, though, an expensive watch snaked around his lean, strong wrist.

'Don't let that get wet!' she exclaimed warningly.

Damos glanced at her. 'Waterproof to three hundred metres,' he said. 'I could wear it scuba diving if I wanted.'

'Do you?' she asked, perching herself on the wide stone rim of the fountain. 'Scuba dive, I mean? Not wear a zillion-euro watch while you do it.'

'No,' he said. He perched himself beside her. 'I haven't the time.'

'That's a shame. Now that you've made money, could you not relax more?'

She'd meant what she'd said. But her thoughts went back to what he'd said about ambition. Maybe he felt he still hadn't made enough money? Maybe he was determined to be richer still? Was he still chasing his next achievement?

A sideways look came her way. 'Isn't that what I'm doing now? Relaxing…taking time out to be a tourist?'

Kassia smiled. 'Well, maybe it will help give you a taste for relaxing more—taking your foot off the business accelerator.'

He didn't answer, only idly laced the water between his fingers. For a few moments longer they went on sitting there, side by side, hands casually stirring the water, hearing birdsong all around them, other visitors wandering past, sunshine bathing them all.

She gazed about her at all the splendour of their surroundings in the summery warmth. This day had come out of nowhere...being here with Damos Kallinikos who, for whatever inexplicable reason, seemed to want to spend it with her. But she wasn't going to question it. All she was going to do was simply enjoy it...

Damos levered himself to his feet. 'Shall we check out the lower water terrace now?' he posed.

Kassia stood up, and they made their way off the upper terrace.

'Apparently, the fountains on the lower terrace are in the style of Bernini's fountain in the Piazza Navona in Rome,' Kassia remarked.

'Have you been to Rome?' Damos asked casually.

He wanted to keep all his conversation with her casual. He'd been unnecessarily intense on the house tour, sounding off about how hard he'd had to work to get where he was today. His own assertion echoed in his head now.

'I made my money honestly.'

Well, it was true, he thought defiantly. He *had* made his money honestly—he had never cheated, or undercut, or been underhand. When the time came he would make

Cosmo a fair offer for his business—once he'd disposed of Yorgos Andrakis's attempt to snap it up, using his own daughter to do so.

Just as you are doing.

The words hung in his head, making him suddenly uneasy.

He dismissed them.

It would stop her father using her, he retorted instantly. And nothing her father wanted would be in Kassia's interest—certainly not being bullied and browbeaten into marrying Cosmo Palandrou.

Whereas what I want is, in fact, in Kassia's interest.

And not just to protect her from her father's ruthless ambitions.

Her words over lunch came back to him. He'd wondered why she did not make more of her appearance, but now he was pretty sure he knew the answer. His mouth tightened. He'd take a bet that Yorgos Andrakis, powerfully built and physically imposing, well used to overbearing other people with his abrupt and hectoring manner, did not like it that his own daughter dwarfed him—it would put his back up straight off. And it sounded as if her mother simply made her even more self-conscious about her slender height.

His glance went to Kassia, walking beside him. She wasn't hunching her shoulders, he noticed. Presumably because he was taller than her and she didn't need to? Her now straight back and shoulders gave a graceful sway to her body as they strolled along…

'A couple of times,' Kassia said.

Damos realised with a start that she was answering his question about whether she'd visited Rome.

'The remains of ancient Rome are very splendid, but they're a thousand years and more later than my period.' She smiled.

'Yet two thousand years ago from the present day?' he commented. He frowned deliberately. 'History does seem to occupy an inordinate length of time,' he said ponderously.

She laughed, and he liked the sound of it.

'And on that profound note,' he said, lightly and self-mockingly, 'shall we head down towards the lake?'

'That would be nice,' she replied politely.

He gave a laugh. 'We don't have to if you don't want to—there's a lot else to see.'

'Well, it's your day out, after all,' she answered. 'I can come here any time, really, whenever I visit my mother, but you might not be in this area again.'

'True,' he murmured.

Truer than she realised…

I'm only here at all because I am in pursuit of you.

And his pursuit of her was for a very specific reason…

He'd said, back there on the upper water terrace, that he was taking today out to relax, but he'd spoken disingenuously. If he had to file this day—this entire trip to the UK—under anything, it would not be 'leisure'. Making up to Kassia Andrakis was serving a business purpose—a clear and unambiguous one.

His glance went to her as they strolled along the winding path leading them towards the lake, his gaze veiled. Yes, he'd forged this acquaintance with Kassia Andrakis for one purpose only.

But is it only one?

The question was in his head, and he could not dismiss it.

Or deny it.

Was his intention to have an affair with her simply a means to thwart her father's plans for her in respect of Cosmo Palandrou? Was it really the only reason he was spending time with her? Or was another reason making itself felt?

Because he was enjoying the day, he realised. Enjoying this leisurely ambling around this magnificent place, seeing the spectacular fruits of one man's towering ambitions. He was enjoying the ease of the day, enjoying feeling as relaxed as he was, and enjoying thinking about something quite other than what usually dominated his thoughts: his endless business concerns.

I'm enjoying being with Kassia.

She was so very different from the women he was used to consorting with. True, if it hadn't been that she was Yorgos Andrakis's daughter he knew he would not have bothered to know her at all. But now that he did…

I like her. I like her company, her conversation. I like her courtesy and her consideration and her knowledge of things I know nothing about, which she makes interesting and easy to enjoy.

And he knew there was something else he liked about her. The fact that she was not indifferent to him.

Oh, he wanted her to be responsive to him—that was essential if he was to have the affair he planned with her. But now he found he wanted it for reasons quite different from that purpose. Reasons he had not expected at all when he'd first engineered an encounter with her. Reasons he knew he had to acknowledge.

Even if she were not Yorgos Andrakis's daughter I would want her to be responsive to me...

His veiled gaze rested on her as they strolled along, chatting about things that seemed easy to chat about, such as the way the gardens had been laid out and what else there was to see. But as it rested on her, he frowned. There was something about Kassia Andrakis that he did *not* want.

I don't want her thinking about herself as she does—with that dismissive criticism of herself, as if she agrees with her parents' verdict on her—as if she sees nothing amiss in the way she remarked, on my yacht, that men only make up to her because of whose daughter she is. I don't like the way she thinks so little of her looks and her appearance.

He did not like that at all.

A sense of irony struck him. Kassia's background might be privileged, but her self-image was anything but. Determination speared through him, and he realised he had just taken on board a new sense of purpose. To reveal to Kassia the beauty that could be hers...

For his own sake, yes—he was honest enough to concede that point—but for something he hadn't thought would matter to him. Now it did.

For her sake too.

CHAPTER FOUR

KASSIA CLIMBED INTO the passenger seat of Damos's hire car and buckled up as he settled himself behind the wheel. Her eyes flickered sideways as he pulled his own seat belt across him and gunned the engine. So, they were heading back into Oxford, where he would drop her off, and then tomorrow she would set off to the Midlands—she'd arranged to stay for a couple of days with an old schoolfriend.

Then she'd probably fly back to Greece.

Taking memories of today back with her. Good memories.

Because today *had* been good—very good.

Spending it with Damos.

Once she'd disciplined herself not to keep stealing glances at him, not to be too aware of just how incredibly attractive he was to her sex, she had settled down to enjoy his company. He'd been easy-going, interested in what they'd talked about, and good-humoured, with a ready smile and a ready laugh. After the lake they'd gone further afield, across the splendid south lawn, exploring more of the vast grounds and gardens, finishing off with coffee at yet another café on the huge estate.

'Tired out?' Damos smiled across at her as they eased their way down the imposing drive towards the main road.

'Good exercise.' She smiled back.

It was only a few miles back into Oxford, so this, she knew, was the end of her day with him. She'd be saying goodbye to him and this time it would be permanent. No more coincidentally running into him again. Oh, he might, perhaps, show up at next season's dig, just to see what his funding might have turned up, but that was about all. Possibly, too, when she was next summoned to Athens by her father, for whatever reason, she just might see Damos around. But he'd doubtless have some glamorous female draped over him…

She felt a pang of sadness well up in her—or something like sadness. She wasn't sure what. All she knew was that she didn't want the day to end.

Just why that was she didn't want to think about. Because what would be the point? She wasn't glamorous, or beautiful, and Damos Kallinikos had only been being friendly, sharing today with her as a convenient but passing companion, for want of anyone else—that was all.

'Well…' he turned on to the road leading back to Oxford '…if you're not too tired, I've another favour to ask you.'

He threw a glance at her, and Kassia looked at him with questioning surprise.

His eyes went back to the road.

'The favour is this,' he said. 'After my meeting yesterday, while you were at your conference, it seems I have an invitation to one of the colleges this evening. It's some kind of shindig—is that the word in English?—where former students who are now influential in the world of business and politics and so on can be wined and dined. Presumably with a view to encouraging them to spend their money and exert their influence on behalf of their old college. My business contact here is one such former student, and he has got the Master to give me an invitation as well.'

His voice took on a sardonic tone.

'It seems one does not have to be an old student to be considered potentially useful to the college providing one has money—even foreign money, like mine. That said, the evening could potentially be useful to me, too, as my business contact tells me that a government trade minister whom it would be helpful for me to know personally will be attending. So...' He glanced at her again. 'Would you be prepared to be my plus one for the evening?'

Kassia looked at him. 'But surely you'll be the guest of your business contact?'

He shook his head, his eyes back on the road. 'Not really. The invitation is from the Master, and it includes a plus one of my own.' He looked at her again as they paused for the traffic lights by the Oxford ring road. 'It would be good if you would perform that office.' He made a slight face. 'It would just make the sociability of it all that much easier.'

His tone grew sardonic again

'As I'm sure you'll appreciate, nothing so vulgar as business or money will be mentioned—this is all about networking, socialising, making introductions and so on. It's a social investment, I suppose—and my arriving with a plus one would play to that.' He paused again. 'What do you say?'

Strange feelings were going through Kassia. It was happening again. A man she barely knew—or, to be fair, had barely known before today—was now making a point of inviting her to spend time with him. But why?

Obviously, as she knew perfectly well, it was not for any of the usual reasons that a man might invite a female out—that thought wasn't even in the running. But did he really want to extend the day they'd spent together into an evening together as well? It seemed he did. And, yes, she could see why—up to a point...

He was speaking again.

'And it's not just any plus one, Kassia. This is your world—academia. You're at home in it in a way that I am not, even though it could prove useful to me in a business sense ultimately. You'll be at ease at an Oxford college social event.'

'I never went to Oxford,' she objected.

'You work in academia—that's my point.'

'In a very junior capacity—'

'Stop making objections!'

There was humour in his voice, but there was something else as well. She could tell. It was determination. He wanted her to say yes. It would suit him for her to do so.

'Look...' he went on. 'On my own, I'm just some self-made Greek business guy, only knowing the world I come from, only knowing the English businessman who arranged this invitation for this evening. With you at my side it would give me something else as well. I've no idea if their professor of ancient history, or whatever, will be there tonight, but just the fact that you can talk on equal terms with other academics—even if you're just a junior one—will help oil wheels. Like I say, this is your world, not mine. You'll be at home here, and that will help me. So, will you come along?'

What he said made sense. OK, so she wasn't an Oxford graduate, but she could hold her head up robustly enough. She'd just been a conference delegate here—she was, in short, *bona fide* in the world he was entering this evening.

But then a real objection hit her.

'It's going to be black tie, isn't it? These formal things always are at Oxford. If so, I haven't got any evening clothes with me,' she said.

The smartest outfit she'd brought with her had been for the pre-conference dinner—a day dress she'd worn with a jacket and low heels. Nothing good enough for a black-tie affair.

'No problem. We're still in time for the shops,' said Damos. 'I'll head for the shopping centre and drop you off. Will that do?'

'Um…yes, thank you,' she said.

'Good. That's settled.'

Satisfaction was clear in Damos's voice.

He crossed the ring road, heading into the city. Beside him, Kassia sat, wondering what she'd let herself in for. But she knew from the way her heart rate had quickened that, whatever the reason Damos Kallinikos wanted her to come with him this evening, she wanted it too.

I don't have to say goodbye to him. Not quite yet…

And her heart rate quickened again.

Damos's mood was good. Very good. He minutely adjusted his bow tie as he gave himself a final glance in the mirror in his hotel room. The car would be here soon, to drive him the short distance to the college hosting the event this evening. He would meet Kassia at the entrance—the college she'd been staying at for her conference was almost next door, so she'd said she'd walk.

He wondered what she'd be looking like…what kind of evening outfit she'd got for herself. But, judging by what he knew, he didn't hope for much.

He was right to do so.

When, some fifteen minutes later, he saw her waiting under the stone arched entrance to the college, he gave an inner sigh. The matronly dress she'd bought for herself did absolutely nothing for her. In a dull shade of dark green, it had a high round neck, a bodice that looked ruched in a bunchy way, and was tightly long-sleeved. Beneath the ruching it dropped widely to her ankles, looking as if it were a size too large for her. Her hair was still in its knot on the back of her head, and she still had not used any make-up.

Frustration stabbed through him, laced with determination. He would change Kassia's low self-image of herself… make her realise her potential… But not tonight. Tonight was about getting to third base with her.

He smiled warmly as he came up to her. 'Dead on time,' he greeted her. 'Excellent.'

'Well, I'm right next door after all,' she replied.

They walked forward under the archway, nodding at the college official on duty. A reception table was set out just beyond, and Damos gave his name and hers. Beyond, in the grassy quad, guests were already gathering. The evening was warm, and the clink of glasses and the chatter of conversation reached across to them. Around the edges the ancient college guarded this central area, in one corner of which a string quartet was playing.

'Shall we?' said Damos, holding his arm out to Kassia.

She hesitated slightly before placing her hand on his sleeve, but then did it anyway. Damos looked around him. The college was incredibly atmospheric in the evening light—the golden stone of the buildings, the dark green of the quad's pristine lawn, the strains of classical music wafting over the space… As they neared where the other guests were gathered he saw that several tables with white linen tablecloths were laden with glasses and bottles, serving staff behind them.

'Now, I do think on a quintessentially traditional occasion such as this clearly is that champagne is in order,' Damos said, and smiled, accepting a glass from one of the servers and handing it to Kassia.

She made no demur, and he took a glass for himself as well, strolling on with her on his arm. She wore some kind of perfume, he noticed—nothing heavy, but something light and floral. It mingled, he thought, with the scent of jasmine descending from climbers festooning one area of the college walls.

'Ah, there you are!'

A voice hailed him, and the man who was his business contact here stepped out of a knot of people. Introductions were made and, just as Damos had foretold, Kassia was quite able to hold her own as she was introduced to college dons, answering questions about her own specialist field and then moving the conversation on. Canapes circulated, along with more champagne, and Damos relaxed into the occasion.

At some point he was duly introduced to the Master who—again as he had foretold—was more than happy to

make the acquaintance of a wealthy guest, albeit a foreigner.
The Master then introduced him to the government minister, and pleasantries were exchanged, potential future con-
tacts made which might well prove useful at some point.
And then there was a general move into dinner.

'High Table,' murmured Kassia, glancing around the
ancient dining hall, panelled and resplendent, as they took
their places once the Master, dons and the ministerial guest
of honour had taken theirs and a long Latin grace had been
intoned. 'We had nothing like this at my northern redbrick!'

She spoke humorously, but Damos looked at her. 'Do
you wish you had been a student here?'

She shook her head. 'I didn't apply,' she said cheerfully.

'Why not?' Damos frowned.

'Because I knew I wasn't Oxbridge material, and so did
my teachers. It doesn't bother me,' she said with a smile.
'I've always accepted my limitations—including intellec-
tual.'

She shook out her napkin and draped it across her lap,
pouring herself some water and replying politely to a re-
mark addressed to her by one of the other diners. Damos
let his eyes rest on her, her words resonating in his head. A
new determination fired in him—there were some limitations she should not accept. He did not want her to. They
were holding her back.

*Holding her back from responding to me as I want her
to.*

Because he could tell that she was doing so. Oh, she
might be far more at ease in his company now—their day
out together at Blenheim had seen to that—and she'd lost
any last trace of awkwardness or hesitation with him, but

she was still treating him as if she were holding back from regarding him as anyone but a pleasant companion.

Yet the signs were there that that was just not so. There were too many tiny but telltale giveaways. The way she moved away from him slightly if he was too close...the way she threw little glances at him when she thought he would not notice...the way a faint colour would run into her cheeks if he held eye contact with her too long.

He knew the signs.

But what he definitely wasn't doing was responding to them. He wasn't coming on to her in the slightest. Not yet. If he did, she'd shy away. He knew it with every instinct. No, all he could do for now was continue as he was, making himself pleasant, easy company for her, enjoying the evening. And it was certainly an evening to remember.

Kassia was clearly enjoying it too, with the candlelight playing on her face as the courses were served, the wine was poured, and all the arcane rituals observed—including having everyone remove themselves to another panelled room to partake of a second dessert, comprising cheese, sweetmeats, fruit and choices of port, liqueurs and sweet wines. Damos couldn't decide whether to be impressed or amused...

'Hang on to your napkin!' Kassia whispered. 'We're supposed to mingle with new people now.'

They did, one of whom was a classicist, and Damos held back and let Kassia engage with him happily on a comparison of Mycenaean, Homeric and Classical Attic Greek. She was in her element, he could see, and that same silvery glow was in her expressive, grey-blue eyes as he'd seen when she'd enthused about the broken bits of pots she spent her time uncovering.

He sat quietly and watched. Even in that dress that did nothing for her, with her severe hairstyle and unmade-up face, there was still something about her…something that made him want to go on looking at her. Hearing her voice… Being close to her…

He realised he was being addressed by the classicist, who was asking him if he, too, were an archaeologist.

He shook his head. 'But I've agreed to sponsor Kassia's museum's dig next season, if that exonerates me,' he said, and smiled.

'Oh, indeed,' came the reply. 'I would keep quiet about that here, though, if I were you. Archaeology is an expensive business, and always hungry for funding! You'll be plagued to death if word gets out!'

Damos gave the expected laugh, but his thoughts were sober. He had sponsored Dr Michaelis's excavation not out of the slightest interest in archaeology, but for the sole purpose of engineering an introduction to Kassia. Moving in on her. Lining her up to clear the path for him to acquire Cosmo Palandrou's logistics company. It would significantly enlarge his own business interests, increasing his own wealth yet more, the way he'd striven to do all his life, from poverty to riches, in order to fulfil his driving, relentless ambition…

Yet somehow, here and now, with Kassia beside him in this historic, atmospheric panelled room at this ancient Oxford college, having spent the day with her among the baroque splendours of Blenheim in the heart of England, that all seemed very far away.

But I am only here with her to drive my purpose forward. That is my only reason for being here at all.

He must not forget it. Whatever his thoughts about Kassia now, they did not obviate his intention in that respect. Yes, he might have come to be drawn to her, irrespective of who she was, but for all that she remained Yorgos Andrakis's daughter—and it was for that reason alone that he had an interest in her.

Then tell her.

The words were in his head out of nowhere. Stark and bare. Impelling.

Tell her. Tell her what you suspect her father is up to. Tell her that the sure-fire way to stop him in his tracks is to let Cosmo Palandrou see you are involved with her. Just tell her that. It's all you have to do.

But if he did…?

More words came. Words he could not silence, or dispute, or deny.

How do you know what her reaction will be?

He didn't—that was the blunt answer.

She might not believe him…might think he was exaggerating…might dismiss it out of hand. He could feel tension tighten across his shoulders as he drove the logic forward. And even if she didn't—even if she did credit what he was telling her—why should she go along with his method of disposing of her father's plans? She might think it quite unnecessary—might believe that all she had to do was tell her father she didn't want to marry Cosmo. And maybe, for all his bullying ways, Yorgos Andrakis wouldn't succeed in pressurising her to do his will.

But he'll keep that from Cosmo for as long as he can. He'll drag things out…tell Cosmo she'll come round…keep him hopeful. And that means Cosmo won't be open to any

other offers—including mine. And while it drags on other
buyers might get wind of what's going on, see that Cosmo's
company is vulnerable and start to circle too. And then
there'll be a bidding war, pushing the price up.

He drew a breath. No, the surest way to outmanoeuvre
Yorgos Andrakis and make the way clear for his own bid
for Cosmo's business was to spike his guns. By making
Cosmo not want to marry Kassia at all—putting him off
completely by the means he'd determined on right from
the start. Getting to Kassia first himself, thereby putting
Cosmo off for good—the way he was already doing.

His eyes rested on her. She was sipping her sweet wine
and still discussing Ancient Greece with her fellow academic. Damos was all too darkly conscious that she was
oblivious to what was going through his head. To the decision he was coming to—the only safe one to make.

He felt himself steel.

It's just too risky to tell her.

And there was no need to, he reminded himself tightly.
No need to do anything other than what he was already
doing. Keep going on the path he had selected.

It was working, and it would go on working—right to
the end.

And by then…

Kassia will be mine.

He felt his thoughts soften, his eyes lighten, the tension
in his shoulders ease. He joined in with the conversation
again, taking a refill of port as it circulated, feeling its
richness mellowing him even more. The evening wore on,
and he knew he was enjoying it—not just because of being
here, but because he was sharing the evening with Kassia.

He said as much to her as, with the guests finally dispersing, they strolled across the quad.

'Are you glad you came?' he asked. 'Because I am—very glad. It wouldn't have been the same without you.'

His smile on her was warm.

'It was a unique experience,' she answered, her voice just as warm. 'Thank you for taking me.'

'It was,' he assured her, 'my pleasure.'

And that, he knew with certainty, was completely true.

She made the evening for me...

It was a thought to warm him—much more than thinking about Cosmo Palandrou or Yorgos Andrakis and all that went with them. He set that determinedly aside, turning instead to Kassia.

'I'll walk you back,' he said.

He hadn't bothered to order another car—the distance to his hotel was not far, and the college Kassia was staying at was next door.

At the entrance, he paused, looking down at her. She was wearing heels, but very low, and her shoes, he'd noticed with the same condemnation he'd reserved for the dress she was wearing, were serviceable rather than elegant. She was still a few inches shorter than he was, though, and she was looking up at him perforce.

In the dim light he thought he saw something move in her eyes. On impulse, he reached for her hand. He lifted it to his mouth, grazing her knuckles lightly...so lightly. He felt her hand tremble in his as he straightened. He smiled down at her. A warm, encompassing smile.

'For me,' he said, 'it's been a memorable evening—quite

an experience! And a great day out seeing Blenheim too. Thank you for making both so special.'

He released her hand and looked down at her a moment longer. She was gazing up at him, lips slightly parted, and there was something in her eyes he had not seen till now. Something wide and wondering.

Almost, he started to lower his head to hers. Then he halted. Instead, he glanced through the entrance to the college where she was staying. The night porter was visible at his desk, clearly able to see them. Damos took a step back.

'Goodnight, Kassia,' he said, still holding her eyes. 'Sleep well. And, again, thank you...'

He turned away, heading back down the road. He had the distinct feeling that Kassia had not moved. That she was watching him walk away from her. As if she did not want him to.

It was good to know. Very good. For reasons he did not entirely wish to acknowledge. Conflicting reasons...

He gave a shake of his head. But those reasons needn't be conflicting—that was the beauty of it. He could want Kassia for herself and for the reason he had set out to want her in the first place.

There is no conflict between them.

He kept the words in his head, walking on back to his hotel. It was time to think of what his next step would be. It would be his home run...

Making Kassia his.

CHAPTER FIVE

KASSIA LET HERSELF into her room, still in a daze. On her bare hand she could still feel the light…oh, so light imprint of Damos taking it in his and kissing it. Such an old-fashioned gesture—and yet now she could understand why Victorian maidens had swooned over it.

For just a moment she let herself relive it, feel again the warm clasp of his hand, the cool touch of his lips…

She gave herself a mental shake. She had no business reacting like this, she told herself sternly. No business wanting to read anything into it.

Deliberately, she moved her eyes to the mirror over the chest of drawers, made herself look at her reflection. Really look.

No, she had not turned into some fairytale princess whose hand a man like Damos Kallinikos—God's gift to women if any man was ever rated so!—would be kissing for any romantic purposes.

I'm still exactly the same as I always have been and always will be. Whether I'm in evening dress, or day wear, looking smart or looking casual, it makes no difference at all.

Whether her father told her brutally and viciously, or her

mother sighingly and sympathetically, it did not—could not—alter what she was seeing in the mirror. What she had always seen…all her life.

She turned away, blinking a little. Damos Kallinikos had kissed her hand because he was being *gallant*—that old-fashioned Continental term for old-fashioned courtesy. He would have done as much had she been an old lady of eighty.

She took another breath, steadying herself. There was no point yearning to be some imaginary glamorous beauty like the kind Damos Kallinikos usually hung out with, because she wasn't. And that was that.

With a lift of her chin she reached her hands behind her back, unzipping her gown. She'd bought it in a rush, given the shortage of time, but it had served the purpose. It wasn't glamorous in the least, or even elegant—but then nothing in her wardrobe was.

She made herself ready for bed, regret pulling at her. Regret that the day was over. She would treasure the memory of their day out at Blenheim, and then the entirely unexpected bonus of the evening just ended. Treasure the memory of being with Damos…

It was strange, really, she thought. She and Damos came from such different backgrounds, led such different lives, yet they seemed to get on well together. Once she'd lost her sense of awkwardness with him, and once she'd got her quite irrelevant, if totally predictable female reaction to him under firm control, she had been quite at ease with him.

As she climbed into bed memories of the evening and of the day were still filling her head, vivid in her mind. She lay back, letting them play. Such lovely memories…

She frowned slightly. There had been only one jarring moment—when he'd talked about ambition, defending it, justifying it. Regret at her own reaction plucked at her.

I have no right fearing it has made him like my father. You can be ambitious without being ruthless...without making use of other people for your own ends. Damos wouldn't do that.

She turned out the light, settling down to sleep. Regret was filling her now for quite a different reason. Because her brief time with Damos was now well and truly over. Definitely over.

It was time to go back to her own life—time to let Damos Kallinikos and her brief encounter with him slip into the past.

Damos was driving to London, his mind occupied with considering his next move with Kassia. He knew she was visiting a schoolfriend for the next couple of days. He'd texted her that morning to wish her a pleasant weekend, and to thank her again for the previous day. But she'd also mentioned, when he'd made a carefully casual enquiry at some point during the day, that there was no pressing need for her to get back to Greece—that she still had annual leave accrued if she wanted to take it.

Damos definitely did want her to take it—with him.

But how to achieve it? How to get her to accept from him what he wanted her to? Accept that he wanted more from her than casual company—much, much more.

His brow furrowed and there was a sardonic twist to his mouth. He was not used to having to work to get a woman to accept his interest in her. He'd gone as far as he could in taking his leave of her last night, and his deliberate hand-kiss had made her tremble. Would he have kissed her if the porter hadn't been able to see them? Would that have convinced Kassia of his intentions?

What he needed, he knew, was to get past her defences—the barrier she lived behind. The barrier of her self-deprecating image of herself.

I need to change her mindset...change the way she sees herself...so I can change the way she sees me...

But how to achieve that?

His thoughts ran on as he cruised along the M40 towards London. He had some business to attend to there, but his main focus was going to be Kassia. It needed to be. Reports from Athens were indicating that Yorgos Andrakis and Cosmo Palandrou were definitely getting together... spending time with each other. Cosmo had apparently been a guest aboard Yorgos's mega yacht—absently Damos recalled Kassia's pungent criticism of it as a monstrosity—and they'd been seen lunching together a couple of times as well. Yorgos was moving things along.

And so must I. I have a limited window of opportunity.

He had the weekend in which to come up with a sure-fire way to seize it.

And by Sunday he knew just what he was going to do.

It would work perfectly...

Just perfectly.

Kassia was out in the garden of her mother and stepfather's house. It was manicured to within an inch of its life, with pristine flowerbeds, a clipped lawn, and an azure swimming pool glinting to one side. The pool looked tempting, even in the slightly cooler temperatures the weekend had brought after the run of hot weather. She would have a dip later.

She was here on impulse. An impulse she didn't quite want to admit to. It had been good, spending the weekend with her friend, but now she was at a loose end. Really, she should head back to Greece—there was nothing to keep her in the UK. But she was conscious of a reluctance to do so—conscious of a reluctance to admit the reason for her reluctance.

She wanted there to be something to keep her in the UK. Or rather some*one*. She knew she was being stupid—ridiculously so—and she knew it was pointless to be so stupid. Knew there was no reason—*none*—for thinking that maybe, just maybe, Damos might get in touch again.

Because why should he? She'd been convenient to him in Oxford—pleasant enough company for Blenheim, useful in her own way for the college dinner. But now he'd gone to London, as he'd said in passing that he would be, and given absolutely no indication that he expected to see her again at any time. That he had any interest in seeing her again.

She gave a sigh, and then gave herself a mental shake. This was absurd. There was no point hanging around like this. Her mother and stepfather were happily on holiday in Spain, and although they were fine with her staying at their Cotswolds house, what on earth was she here for all on her own?

It was pointless—just as pointless as staying on in the UK.

She reached for her phone. She would check the flights and book one for tomorrow. Then she'd text Dr Michaelis to say she'd be back at work this week and defer the rest of her leave till later.

She was just about to search for flights when an incoming call flashed up on her phone.

She froze. It was Damos.

Damos kept his voice smooth. 'Kassia. Hi. How did your weekend go? Well, I hope? Whereabouts are you now? Do you still happen to be in the UK?'

She took a moment to answer.

He felt himself tense.

'Um…yes. I'm at my mother's house. But she's not here. She and my stepfather are in Spain. I'm just…well, just about to book my flight back to Athens.'

'Do you have to get back?' he asked.

Again she took a moment to answer, and again he felt himself tense.

'Er…no, not really.'

Damos felt his tension drop a level.

'In which case, I'll come right out with it. Could I possibly persuade you to do me yet another favour?'

He kept his voice light—deliberately so. She was back to sounding awkward again, and he wanted that gone. Wanted her to relax with him. But there was something else in her voice too. Something that his masculine senses were indicating that he definitely wanted to be there.

She is glad that I have phoned her.

'It's a bit of an ask,' he went on, 'but I need another plus one. You were so kind last week, to be that at the college dinner, and I was wondering if I could prevail upon you a second time.' He paused. 'Let me explain.'

She didn't say anything, so he went on. He needed this to sound plausible—genuine.

'I'm in London and, rather like in Oxford, I've been invited out of the blue to an evening affair.' He made his voice dry, and deliberately humorous. 'It seems that wealthy Greek businessmen are currently in high demand! Anyway, as in Oxford, it would be good for me to arrive with a plus one. So, I'm afraid I immediately thought of you.' He made his voice humorously apologetic now. 'What do you say? It's the day after tomorrow. You'd enjoy it, I'm sure—it's at the Viscari St James, up on the roof garden, so we must hope it doesn't rain.' He paused again. 'What do you say? Can I persuade you to rescue me yet again? I don't want to hassle you, but I'd be really grateful. Of course, if you don't want to I understand completely, and can only apologise for importuning you.'

It was a classic negotiating technique—putting something forward, then seeming to withdraw it.

'It isn't "importuning" me,' she responded. 'Only… Well…um…if you really think…?'

He moved in for the close. 'Kassia, thank you! I'm so grateful. OK… What would be involved is this: I'll send a car for you, the day after tomorrow, then there will be the evening function and a night at the hotel. Of course I'll be covering all expenses. Would that suit? I can't thank you enough. I'm just going to need the address of your mother's house…'

He had it already, but she would not know that.

She gave it to him, somewhat falteringly.

'Great,' he said. 'Look—do forgive me—there's an incoming call from Athens that I need to take. I'm so sorry. But, Kassia—*thank you*!'

He rang off. There was no incoming call, but he didn't want her having second thoughts. He put his phone away, crossed to the sideboard in his hotel suite, and poured himself a beer from the fridge. Relief was filling him. She might have turned him down…might have had other commitments. But she hadn't. She'd agreed to what he wanted.

The ice-cold beer slid down his throat as he took a long draught of it.

And what he wanted was to see her again. As soon as he could…

Oh, he wanted her to fall in with his plans—wanted all of that—but he wanted more, too. A lot more…

He took another, more leisurely draught of his beer.

Of that he was quite, quite certain. Because against all his expectations, all his assumptions, Kassia Andrakis had become more than just a means to an end. She was an end in herself. A very desirable end.

When she had become so, he didn't know. Sometime during that day at Blenheim, or that evening at the college dinner. Sometime when he'd found himself reacting against her downplaying of herself, her passive acceptance of herself as someone men would not be attracted to, when all along…

I know I can show her herself differently, teach her to think well of herself, not ill.

And now he had the opportunity to do just that. The perfect opportunity. It could not have worked out better.

He smiled to himself, finishing his beer, and set aside the empty glass, anticipation filling him. And impatience.

He wanted Kassia with him already.

The rest of the day, and the whole of tomorrow, stretched glaringly, emptily, frustratingly ahead.

CHAPTER SIX

KASSIA LOOKED OUT of the window of the car—a sleek, black expensive model—which had arrived that morning at her mother's house and conveyed her to London. But not to the Hotel Viscari. She looked out again, puzzled. The chauffeur had pulled up against the kerb and was now opening her door. She got out, surprise and confusion in her face. They were outside a famous and very expensive department store in Knightsbridge.

What on earth...?

Her phone buzzed and, still confused, she got it out of her bag to answer it.

It was Damos.

'Kassia? Don't move. I'll be there in a moment.'

Even as he spoke she saw him coming out of the store. Striding towards her. As she saw him she felt her pulse give a kick. She tried to crush it down, but it was a kick all the same.

One she knew she must not feel.

Because from the moment Damos had hung up the phone the day before yesterday she'd known she should have said no to him. Her reaction to his call had told her that—warning her in the way her pulse had quickened, the way gladness had warmed through her just at hearing his voice again. It was pointless to react like that when she was just not the kind of woman a man like Damos Kallinikos would ever think of in the way that she or any other female would love him to...

She sighed inwardly. Yet she'd said yes to him all the same. Said yes because it would be another chance to see him again when she'd thought she never would. How could she have turned it down, pointless though it was? Pointless though it could only ever be?

But now, as he strode up to her, a smile slanting across his face, she felt that betraying kick in her pulse come again, felt her gaze cling to him. And she knew that she was glad—so glad—to have said yes to him. And if it seemed odd—unlikely, even—that he didn't have anyone better than her to invite tonight, given that this was not provincial Oxford but the metropolis, where surely he must know more people...well, she just didn't care. There might be all sorts of reasons she didn't know about as to why he found it more convenient that she should accompany him tonight, and she knew she did not want to question it. Only to be glad of it.

Her own face broke into a warm smile in response to his and she knew her heart rate was quickening. Just seeing him again was a thrill. He was looking a million dollars, in a business suit that sheathed his tall, lean frame, and his dark eyes were as warm as his smile, doing such things to her composure...

He came up to her, greeted her, his voice as warm and welcoming as his smile, and then turned his attention to the driver.

'I'll be about five minutes,' he said.

Then he took Kassia's elbow. His touch was light, but it only added to the hollowing out inside her as he guided her towards the store's entrance.

'Damos, I don't understand. What are we doing here?'

She knew there was confusion was in her voice, as well as that hollowing in her stomach, that kick in her pulse.

He paused, turning to her. 'What I didn't get a chance to tell you on the phone,' he said, 'was that this affair tonight is themed. Thirties Art Deco. Guests are asked to dress accordingly. I've ordered a thirties-style tuxedo for myself, but you'll need something appropriate too. Don't worry...' He smiled reassuringly. 'It's all taken care of. I just have to hand you over, and the specialists here will do the rest.'

He guided her inside the store, towards a bank of elevators.

'But I brought the dress I wore to the college dinner...' Kassia said helplessly.

Damos shook his head. 'Not nearly Art Deco enough,' he said, mentally casting the frumpy green dress into the nearest bin. He ushered her into an elevator. 'All the styling will be taken care of, and of course I'll be covering the cost. All you have to do,' he said, his smile warmer than ever, his eyes warmer still, 'is relax and enjoy.'

Kassia felt breathless—for so many reasons. At seeing Damos again...feeling the warmth of his smile on her... the warmth of his dark eyes on her. But for more as well. She was being whirled away...taken over...by Damos...

The elevator soared upwards, making Kassia feel even more breathless, and she was still breathless when the doors sliced open and Damos ushered her out, towards a very elegantly dressed middle-aged woman who had clearly been waiting for them to emerge.

The woman smiled at Kassia. 'If you would care to follow me, madam…?'

Kassia looked helplessly at Damos. He smiled again.

'See you later,' he said. 'The car will bring you and your overnight bag to the Viscari when you're ready.'

He lifted a hand in farewell and stepped back inside the elevator. The doors sliced shut, and he was gone.

Slowly, feeling her heart thumping idiotically, Kassia went after the elegant middle-aged woman to her fate.

I'm having a dress fitted…a nineteen-thirties-style dress. That's all, she told herself.

But that was not all at all…

Damos stood gazing out of the window of his suite at the Viscari. The rooftops of St James's were beyond, the royal palace was just visible, and there were glimpses of St James's Park as well in the early-evening light. One hand was curved around a whisky glass, the other was plunged into the pocket of his trousers. They were a slightly wider cut than he was used to, and the jacket felt and looked different as well—more waisted, with a satin shawl collar, and it was worn over a white backless waistcoat with a vee-shaped notch. His cufflinks were gold—a new purchase for the occasion—and the wings of his shirt points stiff with starch.

But his thoughts were not on his thirties-style evening dress. They were on Kassia's.

It was just perfect that this affair tonight was Art Deco styled—it provided the perfect reason why Kassia should not be in charge of her appearance…the perfect opportunity to indulge her with a makeover.

Anticipation edged in him and he took a mouthful of his whisky, enjoying the fiery warmth of the choice single malt. He did not have long to wait now. The stylist had phoned through to say she was on her way.

He clinked the ice in his glass, suddenly tensing. He had plans for tonight—plans that would bring to fruition what he had set out to achieve since first getting wind of Yorgos Andrakis's intentions for Cosmo Palandrou—and for his daughter. By tomorrow morning those intentions would be ashes. Because by then Kassia Andrakis would not be anyone Cosmo Palandrou could ever want as his bride.

He felt his fingers grip the whisky glass more tightly. Into his head came the words that had come to him over dinner at the Oxford college.

Tell her—tell her how her father wants to use her for his own interests.

And yet again came his negation.

It was too risky…her reaction too uncertain. Not just for her father's plans for her. For his own.

His expression stilled for a moment, becoming shadowed.

There was one risk above all that he knew he was not prepared to take. Not any more.

I don't want her thinking I only want to make her mine to thwart her father's plans.

That might have been true once—but no longer.

I can't have her thinking that.

The certainty that that was not something he could risk filled him. And that, he knew with equal certainty, was why he wanted…needed…her to think differently about herself. To see herself differently. So that his seduction of her—his wooing of her—would be accepted by her for its own sake…for hers and his.

The shadow left his expression. Soon—any moment now—he would have his proof that that was not just possible but irrefutable. Being styled, gowned and adorned the way she would be tonight must show her, once and for all, that she had no need at all to accept the self-imposed limitations which she felt so unnecessarily she had to live by.

I will change all that for her—so that she can know without doubt or any reason not to believe it that I desire her… And that is all that will be needed for us to be the lovers we shall be…

He felt himself relax, easing his shoulders, taking another mouthful of whisky. He turned his head to the rosewood pier table set opposite the sideboard in the suite's reception room, his eyes going to the thin, flat box delivered by secure courier a short while ago.

The final touch for the evening.

His phone pinged and he glanced at it. It was a text from the driver of the car collecting Kassia, telling him she had just arrived. He knocked back the last of his whisky, setting the empty glass on the sideboard, putting away his phone.

In moments, Kassia would be here.

Hungry anticipation speared through him.

He could not wait to see her…

Kassia edged cautiously along the wide back seat of the car that was pulled up outside the Viscari and carefully—very carefully indeed—stepped out. Behind her, the chauffeur touched his cap politely, shut the car door, and got back into the driving seat to pull away again. Kassia realised the doorman was also touching his top hat to her, instructing a bellboy to fetch her bag and convey it to her room, and holding open the wide glass front door of the hotel for her to enter.

Carefully—very carefully indeed—she walked into the foyer.

She was in shock, she knew. Had been in shock since the stylist, surrounded by the bevy of assorted specialists who had been at work on her for three endless hours, had gently turned her around to face the floor-length mirror in the private changing room.

Kassia had stared. So *much* had been done to her. Way before the dress fitting itself. She'd been whisked into a salon to have her hair washed, and a colour rinse put in, then skilfully snipped—not to shorten it, but to trim and shape it. Then some kind of rich product had been smoothed into it, so that now it had been blow-dried it felt no longer lank and limp, but lush and glossy, glowing a deep chestnut.

And it hadn't stopped at her hair. All sorts of peels and wraps and heaven knew what had been applied to her face and throat, until her skin had felt like satin. Her eyebrows had been shaped, her lashes tinted, and then the manicurist had started work on her hands, smoothing in velvety creams and applying nail extensions and dark red varnish. Then had come the face make-up—and finally had come the gown.

Her breath had caught as one of the assistants had brought it in. Its silky, silvery folds had slithered over her head, over the soft satin camisole and stockings into which she'd been helped, and her feet had been slipped into shoes whose heels were higher than anything she was used to.

And when it had all been done, she'd gazed at herself in the mirror.

She had felt disbelief filling her, and shocked amazement—and beneath and above both of those something else. Something that had made her glow from the inside out...

She'd felt her breathing quicken, her pulse quicken, and she could feel it still now, as she walked carefully on the high heels she wasn't used to across the grand marble-floored foyer—busy at this time of the day—looking around for the elevators.

A member of the hotel staff stepped forward.

'May I help you, madam?' he enquired politely.

Kassia murmured the suite number Damos had texted her.

'Of course. This way, if you please.'

She was ushered into a waiting lift, emerging moments later into a wide, thickly carpeted upper lobby, off which suite doors opened. The staff member led her towards the one marked ten and pressed the intercom. A moment later the door buzzed open and he was ushering her inside, withdrawing as Kassia stepped through.

She was in an elegantly appointed reception room and Damos was standing by the window. Looking right at her.

Not moving.

Completely and absolutely still.

But from across the room Kassia could see in his eyes something that suddenly, gloriously, made the glow inside her blaze...

* * *

Damos could not move. Not a muscle. it was impossible even to think of doing so. His entire being was focussed on his gaze, on what he was seeing.

For an endless moment Damos just went on staring. Then: 'You look *sensational*!'

No other word would do. A surge of triumph went through him. He crossed towards her, taking her hands, his eyes alight.

'I knew—*knew* it was possible!'

His eyes worked over her. He thought of the way he'd last seen her. In that concealing, shapeless, doing-nothing-for-her shop-bought dress, with her hair in a stark knot on top of her head and her face bare of make-up.

It was a thousand miles away from the woman who stood there now—a thousand, thousand.

Her evening gown was in a distinctive thirties style, cut on the bias, completely slinky, with narrow shoulder straps, and it pooled at her ankles. It was made of some kind of shimmering, silvery material that reflected the silvery sheen of her eyes—eyes which skilful make-up had now deepened and enhanced. Mascara lengthened her lashes, her cheekbones were sculpted by blusher, and her mouth— oh, her mouth!—was enriched with lush, dark red lipstick. He glanced down at her hands held in his, and saw that it matched her newly manicured nails.

As for her hair—its nondescript light brown had been coloured to a rich chestnut and it was loosened, finally, from its confining knot to sweep, lush and long, around one bare shoulder.

And her figure…

A rush of renewed triumph went through him. Finally he was seeing what her dowdy clothes had so obdurately concealed from him. Her fantastic, slender, racehorse figure, delicately sculpted, graceful and long-limbed.

His hands tightened on hers for a moment.

'I can't get over it,' he said, still sounding stunned. 'Kassia, I can't *believe* you were hiding all this!'

He saw a tremulous smile form at her lips.

'I… I didn't know I was hiding it,' she said.

He gave a laugh, swiftly lifting one of her hands to his mouth, and then the other, then lowering them again.

'Well, one thing is absolutely for sure—you are *never* hiding it again!

He led her forward, releasing one of her hands, admiring the way her walk was swaying now, courtesy of her four-inch heeled silver evening shoes. He turned her towards the mirror over the pier table. Still holding her hand, he looked at their reflections, side by side. He heard her breath catch. Saw her beautiful eyes glow more silver.

'Total thirties Hollywood,' he said. 'The pair of us! We just need to be in black and white!'

Kassia's eyes met his in the mirror. That intense glow was still in them.

'You look amazing yourself,' she said.

Her eyes lingered on him, and he felt another surge of triumph go through him.

'We definitely both look the part,' he agreed. 'Oh, Kassia…' His voice changed. 'I just can't get over how sensational you look!'

'Me neither,' she said. She gave a laugh as tremulous as

her smile had been. 'I'm in shock—I know it. I just didn't realise—'

She broke off, and Damos picked up her words. 'But I did, Kassia,' he said. 'I realised that you simply believed your parents' verdict on you. But don't you see?' His voice changed again. He wanted, *needed* her to understand. 'They judged you by their own standards. Think about it... Your mother is petite and full-figured—you said so. And that, obviously, is the look that drew your father to her. It's the look he likes. But you, Kassia, are like a thoroughbred race-horse!' He gave a laugh, low and triumphant. 'Tonight,' he said to her, 'everyone—and I mean *everyone*!—is going to think I've got the latest supermodel on my arm!'

He squeezed her hand lightly, then let it go. Triumph was still surging through him. He'd wanted so much for Kassia to see herself differently, to be freed of that self-deprecating self-image she'd lived with. And now she was—because surely she could not deny what her own eyes were telling her. It would be impossible to do so—the evidence was right there. And he could tell she was beginning to get used to it, to accept it. She was still gazing at her reflection, glowing at what she was seeing, partly in disbelief, partly simply looking alight with delight.

'Let's have a drink before we head up to the roof terrace,' he said now. 'We've plenty of time. What can I pour you?'

Her gaze dropped from her own reflection as if reluctantly. 'Oh. Um...if there's wine later, then probably just another OJ spritzer is best now.'

'Coming right up,' Damos said, crossing to the sideboard and deftly pouring her a long glass, handing it to her, fixing himself a non-alcoholic mixer. He'd already had a whisky, and alcohol would be flowing tonight. He didn't want to drink too much…

Because there is only one way that I want this night to end.

His eyes went to her again as they clinked glasses, their gazes entwining. He felt his pulse kick…saw the sudden flaring in her eyes…felt his pulse kick harder.

He felt desire creaming in him and he knew, with a surge of triumph that was the strongest yet, that finally Kassia would accept that desire. Would believe it possible.

She cannot deny the beauty that is hers. The beauty that glows in her eyes has been revealed not just to me, but to her.

As he clinked his glass to hers he could see that belief taking a stronger hold yet in her. She was throwing little glances at her reflection, and he saw how doing so brought a curve of delight to her lips, intensifying the silvery sheen of her eyes.

'To tonight,' he said now, his voice low. 'To a wonderful evening!'

Silently he added his own coda.

And to an even more wonderful—wondrous!—night together.

Because one thing was for sure. Tonight, without the slightest doubt, was the night she would become his.

He only had to let his gaze rest on her, drink her in, to tell him why he was so determined on it.

Because any other outcome right now seemed quite, quite impossible…

This feasting of his gaze on her, on all the stunning

beauty that she herself could now finally believe in, would this very evening release her to him.

Kassia was in a dream. A dream of disbelief and delight... delight and disbelief. But disbelief was impossible—every glance at her reflection told her that.

And more than her own reflection was the look in Damos's eyes as he gazed at her.

It was the look she had longed to see but never thought to. Had thought it pointless to yearn for. Never thought it possible.

But now...now it is.

She felt her heart rate give yet another skip, her breath catch yet again.

Now, thanks to the hours of grooming and pampering and adorning, she could hold her head up and know with the wonderful, heady delight inside her that no longer did she have to hopelessly, resignedly envy that parade of svelte, glamorous beauties the Internet had shown her draped all over Damos Kallinikos. Now she was one of them...

I truly am! I can see it for myself. Staring me in the face...

Her glance went to the mirror again, confirming it. How could it be otherwise when she was in this incredible gown, with her hair, her face, all telling her that now she was just the kind of woman Damos Kallinikos would want at his side?

She felt wonder course through her, hearing his words again. Could it really be that simple? That she had never believed she could look as she so obviously looked now just because her style of beauty was not her parents'? She had just accepted it—accepted their verdict and never tried to do anything with herself, never seen the point of it.

Realisation speared through her. It had taken Damos to see it—to see what she herself had not been able to and to get her to see herself differently.

And he's seeing me differently too...

She knew he was. She could see it in his eyes, in his gaze. A little thrill of new awareness went through her. It was telling her that now he was not seeing her simply as a pleasant companion for a day, an evening...but as someone much more. Wonderfully, thrillingly more...

And if having Damos smile at her had been able to make the colour run into her cheeks simply because they were enjoying their day together at Blenheim, or their evening at the Oxford college, now there was a new warmth in his eyes, a different warmth, and it was as if she, too, could have the same warmth in her own eyes. For the same reason.

I don't have to hide it any longer...conceal it—deny it.

She felt a shimmer deep inside. Felt her breath catch. Delight lit up within her—more than delight, oh, deliciously more. She smiled. She could not help it. The smile played at her mouth and she was dazed with it...dazed with the glorious new knowledge shimmering through her.

Damos was setting down his glass, picking up a flat case lying on the pier table, flicking it open.

'Sensational though you are, you need just one more adornment,' he said.

Kassia's eyes widened. Inside the case was a glittering loop—a single strand diamond necklace—and two equally glittering brooches in distinctive Art Deco style.

'They're originals from the period. I hired them for to-night,' he told her.

He picked up the brooches, holding them out to her, and Kassia took one, turning towards the mirror again to fasten it very carefully at the base of one of the evening dress's straps, and then do likewise with the other.

'And now the necklace,' said Damos.

He was standing behind her and he lifted the glittering strand into his hands, bringing it forward to loop it around her throat, carefully smoothing aside the fall of her hair. The stones felt cold on her skin—but his fingers, deftly fastening the necklace, were warm.

That deep, delicious shimmer inside her came again.

He stood back, his hands resting lightly on her upper arms, his palms warm. She could catch the tang of his aftershave, could feel his hands lying so devastatingly on her bare arms.

The shimmer inside her intensified as they gazed at themselves reflected in the mirror in front of them.

'How incredibly beautiful you are, Kassia,' she heard him say.

His voice was a husk, and his eyes...oh, his eyes...were drinking in her reflection. As she was drinking in his.

She felt faintness drum through her. Did she sway? She didn't know. Knew only that Damos was bending his head towards her, dipping it to the curve of her bared shoulder. The sweep of her hair was heavy around her other shoulder as she felt his mouth graze her skin softly, sensuously. The touch of his hands was so light...

She felt weakness wash through her, her eyelids dipping.

He straightened, and a slow, intimate smile curved his mouth as he held her gaze again in their reflection.

'My beautiful, beautiful Kassia,' he said.

And in his voice, warm and husky, was surely all that she could ever have longed to hear and never thought she could.

But she did tonight. Oh, tonight—thanks to the incredible, fantastic transformation that had been wrought upon her—she knew that the reflection of that other woman in the mirror was truly herself...all her...

And it was a wonder beyond all wonders that it should be so...

She held his gaze in the mirror, her eyes twining with his. The breath was stilled in her lungs.

And then Damos was letting his hands fall from her, holding out his arm to her in a stately fashion.

'Time for our evening to begin,' he said, and his smile reached to her, warm and inviting.

Her own smile answered his. Just as warm. Just as inviting.

She placed her crimson-tipped hand over his sleeve.

'Oh, yes...' she breathed. 'Oh, *yes*...'

Damos strolled forward. The rooftop garden of the Viscari St James was *en fête* indeed. Lights glittered from the perimeter trees, glowed from the undergrowth, festooned the paved terrace in front of the glass-fronted, glass-roofed restaurant to one side of the space.

'It's like fairyland!' Kassia exclaimed.

Her hand was still resting on his sleeve, and he could feel her leaning on him slightly. Maybe those four-inch heels were taking some getting used to. Or maybe she was a little nervous?

As they'd emerged on to the roof terrace level, already thronged with guests, he'd felt her tense for a moment. Maybe she was self-conscious about her sensational new appearance? She was certainly drawing eyes—just as he had said she would. Heads were turning as they walked out into the warm evening air to take in the amazing roof garden.

Whatever the reason, he liked the feeling of her leaning on him, letting him support her. They were, he knew, perfectly matched as a couple. Even in heels she was still a tad below his height, and so incredibly slender, her racehorse figure sheathed in the fantastic gown skimming her body, her bare sculpted shoulders a work of art in their own right.

A sense of possessiveness fused through him and he drew her little more closely against him. She was here, with him, for this evening.

And for the night ahead.

Because there could be no other way to end the evening…

Certainty filled him. Never had he been more certain, more sure, that *this* was what he wanted most in all the world.

Kassia—with him.

How far we've come…

His thoughts reached back to his first glimpse of her, crouched down in that trench, head bowed over her work, teasing out that bit of broken pottery in her baggy, dusty work clothes, her face flushed with heat and dabbed with earth, her hair clamped to the back of her neck, with loose, damp strands around her face. How little he had thought of her then except as someone he must engineer an acquaintance with…get to know without having the faintest interest in her personally. Simply because she was Kassia Andrakis.

How totally different it was now.

Totally.

Oh, she was Kassia Andrakis still, but as they stood together, admiring the scene before them, the only thing he cared about was that she was Kassia.

He felt desire course through him again as he caught the scent of her perfume, felt the warmth of her tall, graceful body half leaning against his. Filling his senses.

A server was circulating with trays of drinks, and he helped himself to two flutes of champagne, passing one to Kassia, who took it, bringing her gaze from the roof garden back to him. Their eyes met and melded.

'To a memorable evening,' Damos murmured, clinking his glass gently against hers and then lifting it to his mouth. She did likewise, almost in an echo of his gesture. They were still holding each other's eyes.

It seemed to Damos that suddenly everyone else around them had vanished…

Then a voice broke the moment.

'Damos! Good to see you. Very glad you made it.'

A couple were coming up to them—the Cardmans, London acquaintances of his, through whom he was here tonight.

He greeted them smoothly, introducing Kassia to them, and the Cardmans to her in return.

'Charles is in shipping too—a yacht broker,' he said, explaining the connection.

Charles Cardman's wife turned her attention to Kassia. 'Have you known Damos long?' she asked.

She was probing—it was pretty obvious to Damos.

'Not very,' Kassia answered with a polite smile, unfazed by the question.

'What brings you to London?' Charles Cardman asked conversationally.

'I was in Oxford for a conference and bumped into Damos there. He very kindly asked me along tonight. It's quite amazing, this roof garden! I've never seen it before, and it certainly takes the breath away.'

'Conference?' Valerie Cardman probed.

A good few years younger than her husband, she was nevertheless older than Kassia. She was very good-looking, but Kassia was outshining her hands down. Maybe Valerie Cardman did not like that, thought Damos a touch cynically.

'Oh…um…yes—Ancient Greece,' Kassia said politely. 'I'm an archaeologist.'

Charles Cardman gave a bark of laughter. 'I thought archaeologists were all fusty, musty and dusty!'

'Not this one,' Damos supplied smoothly.

He changed the subject, asking Charles something about the business. Valerie Cardman focussed on Kassia, and as Charles answered his enquiry Damos heard her asking where she had got her retro-style gown.

He heard Kassia name the department store, adding, 'Damos kindly sorted it all out for me. I hadn't got anything suitable with me. It's incredibly slinky, isn't it? I don't know how those Hollywood actresses managed to breathe—I barely can! Yours is gorgeous—like that fabulous one with feathers Ginger Rogers wears in that movie when she and

Fred Astaire are dancing together out on a terrace by moon-light. And you've got her amazing figure too! I'm all up and down—not in and out!'

Covertly, Damos glanced at Valerie as he chatted to her husband. Valerie was preening.

'That's exactly the effect I was after!' she exclaimed, pleased. 'Tell me, do you dance? There's going to be dancing later—not modern stuff, but proper ballroom dancing.'

Kassia shook her head. 'Not in the slightest,' she said ruefully. 'What about you?'

'Oh, I used to be a professional dancer,' Valerie said airily.

'How wonderful! No wonder you're channelling Ginger Rogers tonight!' said Kassia.

With a start of surprise Damos heard genuine admiration in Kassia's voice, and he heard Valerie laugh, pleased.

'How she ever did those amazing routines in high heels I just don't know,' Kassia was saying now. 'I can barely walk in these heels, let alone dance in them! With my beanpole height I'm far more used to flats and being…' she gave a laugh '…just as fusty, musty and dusty as your husband says! This is a real night out for me.'

'Oh, you get used to heels—and to dancing backwards,' Valerie was saying airily. 'It takes core strength, though. And good balance.'

'I can imagine… And it must need so much training and discipline.'

'Years,' agreed Valerie.

'And talent,' her husband put in at this point, smiling benignly at her.

His wife laughed, pleased at the compliment.

Conversation became general, and Damos realised that Kassia was getting on with Valerie in a way he had just not envisaged.

Maybe I'm only used to women competing with each other...seeing each other as rivals.

Kassia wasn't like that—and he could see she had effortlessly disarmed Charles Cardman's wife just by being natural and friendly. She'd got on just as easily at the college dinner, too, adapting her conversation to whoever she was talking to, male or female. Asking them questions... showing an interest.

Most of the females he was used to going out with were only interested in themselves, he thought mordantly. Kassia was completely different...

It was yet another reason for liking her, and for liking being with her. And he acknowledged that her interest in other people, in subjects he had never bothered to care about, had been steadily broadening his own horizons, too.

In the long slog of the years it had taken him to turn himself from deckhand to wealthy businessman he had been tunnel-visioned. Concentrating on one subject only—making money, and then making more money. It had absorbed his life, and everything had been dedicated to that end—dedicated to improving things for himself. Even his romances, such as they were, were always with women who could play to that purpose, add to his image of success and wealth. Whether he liked them or not had never been relevant to his spending time with them.

His eyes shadowed for a moment. When he had first engineered his encounter with Kassia that had been his attitude towards her, too. She herself had not been important—only whose daughter she was. Thoughts moved within him—thoughts he had never experienced before. He had targeted Kassia Andrakis for a very clear purpose of his own that had had nothing to do with either her looks— or lack of them—or her personality. Had she been the very opposite of natural and friendly he'd still have done what he had—and even if the makeover had not been as amazing as it so dazzlingly was.

For a brief moment a frown creased his forehead, as if things were colliding inside him. Confronting each other. Then he shook his head mentally, clearing them away and clearing his expression. He no longer felt that way about Kassia…as if it was only who she was that was important to him.

I've changed.

For a moment it hung there…that simple statement that somehow wasn't simple at all. That was somehow significant…important.

But he did not yet know how he had changed—how it was important…

His eyes went to Kassia, still talking to the Cardmans about ballroom dancing and what they might expect later on, Her beautiful eyes were alight, her face animated. Something swept through him, powerful and strange. Something that he did not recognise, did not know. He knew only that it seemed to be possessing him…taking him over…

Charles Cardman turned towards him, breaking the moment. 'What about you, old chap? How's your foxtrot?' he asked genially.

'Non-existent,' he admitted, mentally refocussing with an effort. 'I can probably manage a waltz, but that's about all.'

'Ah, but what tempo?' Valerie challenged. 'Fast or slow?'

'Does it make a difference?' Damos asked, taken aback.

'Oh, yes!'

She launched into technicalities, and Damos held up his hand.

'I'm lost already! I'll just have to lumber around and do my best.' He threw an apologetic look at Kassia. 'I'll try not to step on your toes as well!'

'You'll both be fine,' Valerie said reassuringly. 'Charles and I will dance with each of you first and give you a quick lesson. Charles isn't at all bad for an amateur,' she said fondly, patting her husband's arm approvingly.

Damos smiled, thanking her, but he knew it was not Valerie Cardman he wanted to take into his arms to dance with—it was Kassia.

To feel her in my arms…to hold her…embrace her. She, and she alone, is the only woman I want in my arms. And in my bed. The only woman…

And again that strange, powerful, unknown feeling swept through him.

Possessing him…

CHAPTER SEVEN

KASSIA SMILED DREAMILY as Damos ushered her into the lift.

'What a wonderful, wonderful evening!' she exclaimed.

She meant it—totally. Little fragments of evocative classic songs and melodies from the nineteen-thirties were playing in her head. She hummed aloud now, still smiling. Beside her, Damos gave a low laugh.

She glanced up at him, her eyes and her face aglow. 'Thank you so much for bringing me. I wouldn't have missed it for the world!'

'My pleasure,' he said promptly, and he smiled at her in return.

In her high heels she was very nearly at eye level with him, and it felt strange. At least, she thought wryly, she'd got used to walking in the heels. And dancing too.

Her smile grew dreamier. She'd told Valerie she couldn't dance and it was true. Certainly she hadn't been able to compete against the older woman's professional skill and flair, which had been such that, once the band had struck up after dinner, and the wide doors had been opened to the terrace beyond, the other dancers had given her and her husband all the space they needed to show off their moves.

But the Cardmans had insisted she and Damos take to

the floor as well, each of them, as Valerie had promised, taking a dance with them. So Kassia had tentatively danced with Charles, even though she was a good head taller than him, and accepted his instructions.

She had been aware that her attention was on his wife, in Damos's arms, similarly instructing him. Aware, too, that she did not like to see Damos with another woman...

When the number had ended and another had been struck up it had been a waltz, slow and beguiling. Charles had released her, and Valerie had released Damos. As Damos had turned to Kassia she'd felt a sudden tremor go through her. She'd all but frozen, rooted to the spot as one of his hands clasped hers and the other curved around her waist.

'Put your free hand on my shoulder,' he'd said encouragingly, and gingerly...oh, so gingerly... Kassia had done so, gazing helplessly at him.

Her eyes had gone completely wide, and she'd felt every fibre of her body tensing. To be in Damos's arms like that...

Then the music had swept into its full melody—and Damos had swept her away.

Into heaven. Just...heaven...

The same melody was in her head now, and on her lips, as she gazed dreamily at Damos.

What was happening to her she didn't know—hadn't known since he had swept her across the dance floor, turning her around, and around, and around as they glided away. What her feet had been doing she hadn't the faintest idea—she only knew what her heart rate had done. It had soared like a bird in flight...up, up and away...

She'd felt herself leaning back as they'd turned around the floor, and his hand at her waist had been supportive, and protective, and so much more. So much more than simply the firm clasp of his hand holding hers. So much more than the slight, but oh-so-potent smile he'd bestowed upon her as his eyes had rested on her face, their long lashes half veiling them, but never for a moment concealing what was in them...

She was still floating on air, floating off to heaven...just floating and floating.

The elevator stopped and the doors opened. Damos was ushering her out. His key card was in his hand and he was sliding it into the lock of the door to his suite. And she was going in...not even thinking to ask about her own room...not thinking at all...

Not realising that Damos was closing the door behind him...turning her towards him...and taking her into his arms...

Her mouth was silk. Her lips satin. His own lips only grazed lightly, so very lightly. He was using all his self-control to keep it like that. His arms were around her waist, hands on the rounded swell of her hips. As he lifted his head from hers he smiled that same half-smile he'd used on her as he'd taken her into his arms to dance with her. His eyes poured into hers.

'You have absolutely no idea,' he breathed, 'how much I have been aching to do that.'

She was looking at him with dilated eyes...eyes that had turned as silvery as her gown. There was wonder in them, and more than wonder. She was looking at him in such a way that there was only one thing to do—only one.

He kissed her again. And this time the lightness could

not hold…could not withstand his own desire. Desire that she had inflamed from that first stunned silence as she had walked towards him, her hidden beauty finally revealed to him. Desire that had been building achingly all evening.

Dancing with her had been both bliss and torture—but now the latter was gone and only the former could exist.

And bliss it was.

His hands tightened on her hips and instinctively he drew her closer to him as his kiss deepened. She yielded to both—and it was all he wanted. Her mouth opened to his, and in her throat he heard her give a little helpless moan. It inflamed him more…

Did she realise just how she was arousing him? Well, she would know soon—it would be impossible to deny. And he had no wish to deny it—no intention of doing so. No intention of doing anything at all except what he had been wanting to do all evening.

Her hands had lifted to his shoulders and he could feel, deliciously, the fingers of one hand sneaking around the column of his neck, spearing into his hair as his kiss deepened yet more. And against the wall of his torso he could feel, even more deliciously, her beautiful, shapely breasts… peaking.

Was she aware of that? Well, she would be soon…very, very soon.

He drew back, breathless, his gaze still pouring into hers.

'Come,' he said.

His voice was low, husked, and filled with his own desire. He reached to lift her hand away from his nape, clasping her loosely by the wrist as her other hand fell away and he freed her from his own grasp. For one long, lingering moment he let his gaze feast on her as she gazed back at him, eyes wide, pupils dilated, lips parted and bee-stung, her face filled with wonder and bemusement and so much more.

His mouth curved into that half-smile and he led her to his bedroom.

And to his bed.

Her gown fell from her in a pool of silver at her feet. Beneath she was wearing only a satin camisole and wispy briefs. A confection of lace was all that was keeping her sheer stockings on her thighs. She'd heard Damos's breath catch as he'd slid down the zip at the back of her gown. She could not move—and why should she? For heaven was here, in his gaze upon her.

Desire blazed in his eyes, melting her with its heat. He said something in Greek, too low for her to make out the words. Besides, her blood was singing in her ears, her heart pounding in her breast. Then, abruptly, he was kneeling, and she realised he was unfastening the straps of her heeled sandals. She stepped out of them, her hand automatically going to his shoulder to balance herself. Then his hands were lifting…lifting to where her stockings were fastened. He undid them and one by one…silkily, gorgeously, arousingly…slid them down her limbs, freed her from them. Only then did he get to his feet again.

'Your turn,' he said.

And that half-smile that did such things to her was at his lips again.

She reached forward, sliding her hand between his jacket

and his shirt, moving it up to his shoulder, easing his jacket from him. He caught it as it fell, tossing it carelessly aside to a nearby chair where it hung loosely. Then he lifted her hands to his tie. Carefully, a little frown of concentration on her face, she pulled at the ends, feeling it come away. Then, while her hands were there, she slipped the top button of his dress shirt. And then the next one. And the next…

Sliding her hands under the fine lawn of the dress shirt to the warm, smooth wall of Damos's strong chest beneath, she let her hand splay, easing across languorously. She gave a sigh of pleasure…

As if it had been a signal his hand shot up, fastening around her wrist, and then, without Kassia quite understanding how, he was sweeping her up into his arms and lowering her down upon the bed. He was ripping the rest of his clothes from him. Waistcoat, shirt and tie and all the rest joined the jacket.

Instinctively, she shut her eyes. Damos fully clothed could set her pulse soaring—but Damos *un*clothed…

She felt the mattress give as he came down beside her and heard a low laugh come from him. He leant over her and she opened her eyes again, to look into his. They were looking down at her with a glint in them which was half humour and half something quite, quite different…

'Oh, Kassia—so shy?'

She gazed up at him wide-eyed. Her heart was beating tumultuously, the blood was singing in her ears, and she was filled with wonder…a dazed, almost disbelieving state of bliss. And yet…

She gave a crooked smile.

'I… I think I am,' she answered.

His mouth dropped to hers. Gently, softly. Briefly.

'Leave it to me,' he told her, his voice warm.

Kassia did just that...

And Damos took her to paradise.

Took her there with a slow, seductive touch.

He explored her body with lips and palms and the exquisite expertise of the tips of his fingers, which found every most sensitive, erotic point of her body...

Slowly, sensuously, he ensured she felt every moment for its maximum pleasure. He eased from her the silky camisole, exposing the sweet mounds of her breasts, their peaks cresting as he circled them lazily, arousingly...oh, so exquisitely arousingly... He was teasing, and lingering, and then... Oh, how could it feel so good, so exquisitely delicious, as his mouth lowered first to one ripened breast and then the other and his tongue flicked at her straining, hard-crested nipples until she wanted to cry out with it.

Then, still holding one engorged breast beneath the soft kneading of his palm, he lowered his attentions. His mouth glided down from the shallow vee between her breasts to the flat plane of her abdomen, fastening his other hand around one hip. His mouth glided lower...and lower yet...

The hand at her hip moved to the wisp of her panties, easing along their waistband, gliding them from her body, then returned to where his mouth now was...

A moan broke from her, and she felt her thighs slacken of their own volition. He eased his hand between them, returning his mouth to her bared breast. And from breast to vee a flame started, running through every vein in her body. A flame that was in the tips of his exploring fingers as he reached to find the delicate tissues at the heart of her femininity.

A gasp sounded in her throat and her hands moved to close over his shoulders, to splay out across the nape of his neck. At her breast, at her feminine core, his ministrations drew from her such sensual delight, such an intensity of pleasure, such a deliciously, achingly mounting arousal as she had never known was even possible…

She moaned again, thighs slackening yet more, head turning on the pillow. An ache was building in her—a yearning, a craving—and the incredible, unbelievable sensations he was drawing from her were impossible to endure. It was impossible not to want more…and more, yet more…

Her blood was surging, engorging, swelling and ripening, exciting and arousing, quickening and intensifying. Her vision was dimming, blurring… The world was dimming, blurring…

Because nothing existed…

Nothing at all except…

This.

This, this, this…

This moment, this now, this absolute, total *now*, was sweeping through her, dissolving her, making her molten, liquid, sweeping through her, pouring into every cell of her body, lifting her, lifting her…

Oh, sweet heaven…

Impossible that she should be feeling what she was feeling. Impossible that such pleasure, such bliss, such gorgeous, gorgeous melting, such heat and sweet, sweet fire should be burning through her… Sweeping on and on… endless and consuming…

And then, before she could even become aware of anything else at all except what was possessing her, what she was possessed by, Damos was lifting away from her, lifting away his mouth and his palm and his gliding fingertips. Instead he was lowering himself over her, one hand cradling her beneath her hips, raising her to him as her whole body flamed yet more blazingly. His body fused with hers, filling her, engorging her, melding with her, and around him her body, completed now by his possession, pulsed and melted.

She clung to him, her hands around his shoulders, bowing up towards him as she cried out. He did too—a hoarse tearing of sound—and she knew with the scything knowledge that was in her thighs, tightening against his, to hold him, keep him there, just there, where her body was pulsing against his, drawing him deeper and deeper yet, making her cry out again and again...

She knew that for him, too, it was as it was for her...

Possession and passion...slaking and sating and never, never letting go...not her of him or him of her...

She held him within her, holding him in the cradle of her arms, wrapping his strong, hard body in hers, holding him and holding him even as their bodies cooled and stilled...

She was dazed, breathless, and her heart was hammering yet, pounding within her—echoing, she knew, with a kind of exultation, the pounding of his own heart, beating against hers.

He lifted away from her a little, his torso only, and she felt him drop a shaky hand on her still-flushed cheek, smoothing it softly, gazing down at her with an expression in his eyes that made her breath catch.

'Kassia—'

Her name—that was all—and it was all she wanted to hear.

A smile curved across her mouth, wide and tender and embracing. 'I don't think I'll be shy next time,' she said softly, her gaze clinging to his, that smile still playing on her lips.

A crack of laughter broke from him.

'Dear God, Kassia, if this was you being *shy*...'

He swept her over to her side, still in her embrace, so that his own embrace could tighten. Their thighs tangled now, as they slipped from each other, and he was kissing her now—not with passion, for passion was exhausted, but with a kind of sealing of what had been between them... and a promise, too.

Kassia felt again that catching of her breath in wonder and wonderment. It was a promise of all that was yet to come before the night was over...

Damos lay drowsily and contentedly, Kassia tight in his arms, as daylight finally pricked its way into the room, edging around the drawn curtains. Amazement still possessed him. After the first time he'd set eyes on her, crouched in that dusty trench, could he ever have thought to this moment now? To how it would be for him? For her...?

Yet again that strange, powerful emotion swept through him. He did not know what it was—knew only that it possessed him. Filled his being.

Idly, languorously, he smoothed his hand over her hip as she lay cradled against him. He let his mouth softly kiss her shoulder, snuggled into his, as memory of the night that had just passed played in his head.

A night of passion—oh, such passion!

Kassia had made love without inhibition. He smiled reminiscently at his saying to her, *'If this was you being shy...'* She had given of herself without stint, with an ardent desire that had more than matched his own, that had had her body...her beautiful, slender body...clinging to his in her ecstasy. An ecstasy that had come time and time again...

Perhaps remembering that right now, while she lay cradled against him, was not the wisest thing... The feel of her body tight against his own was having an effect on him that, as full wakefulness came over him, was increasingly impossible to ignore.

His lazy smoothing of her hip moved forward, reached towards the vee of her thighs, and his mouth at her shoulder started to glide, to taste the delicate line of her throat, to tease...to arouse. Even as he himself was aroused...

She stirred in his arms, a little sigh breathing from her, as he nestled the hand at her vee into the contour of her body, trailing his mouth up from her throat to catch at her lips...

His own arousal was growing...intensifying. She was waking too now, half turning in his arms, her mouth moving to his, tasting and teasing, her thighs slackening. Her body was still pressing back against his...knowingly, sensually. He gave a low laugh, luxuriating in her effect on him, and his kiss deepened, no longer teasing and tasting but probing, possessing. And she answered in kind, turning fully now, so that the engorged tips of her already ripening breasts grazed his chest, arousing him yet more.

He gave a growl, sliding his hand around her hip once more to pull her against him, so that the full strength of his arousal was tangible. His thighs moved over hers in possession...his of her...hers of him. Their bodies were fusing yet again, desire crescendoing. He felt her back arch, her thighs strain. Her head was thrown back, the heat of her shuddering climax flushing her skin, her hair a wanton tangle on the pillow as her head threshed from side to side and she cried out with abandon. Then his own moment was upon him, and nothing else in the world existed except Kassia—this amazing, incredible woman who was his...

In a way he had never known she could be.

CHAPTER EIGHT

KASSIA STOOD NEXT to Damos, gazing out over the loch in front of them, a dreamy expression in her eyes. Had she ever dreamt that life could be so wonderful? No, she never had—it would have been impossible that she could ever have dreamt it so. Because never had she dreamt that a man like Damos could be in her life.

But the very expression 'a man *like* Damos' was wrong—it was Damos himself she had never dreamt about.

How wonderful he was! Just wonderful! And since that *wonderful* night she had spent with him her life had been transformed. Transformed into blissful happiness.

She turned to look at him now, her gaze drinking him in. He was standing beside her on the beach, binoculars pressed to his eyes, watching a large bird soaring over the forested far shore, behind which the ground rose upwards to a high, rounded ben.

She felt her heart give a little skip, the way it always did when she looked at Damos.

Is this really real...me being here with him?

That first morning, surfacing from that wonderful night, it had seemed almost a dream to her. But it was a dream he'd made real—was making real every day.

They'd spent all that first day together in his suite—in his bed—dining in as well. It had been another whole day until they'd surfaced.

'Let's get out of London,' he had said. *'I want you all to myself—somewhere miles and miles from anywhere.'*

Kassia couldn't have agreed more. She wanted Damos all to herself as well.

The Highlands of Scotland fitted the bill perfectly. Here, standing on the stony little beach, with the dark water of the narrow loch lapping gently near their feet, the only dwelling for miles around was the place where they were staying.

A castle—a genuine Scottish castle. Theirs for a whole fortnight.

It was only a small one—a solid, stone-built keep, set back from the loch's edge. It had an imposing entrance hall upon whose walls was a fearsome display of weaponry, a gracious drawing room with a cavernous fireplace and comfortable tartan sofas, an elegant panelled dining room with an oak table and furniture, and upstairs a bedroom with a four-poster bed with velvet hangings, and cosy sheepskins on the polished wooden floor.

The castle might be ancient, but it came with modern plumbing and central heating—and a married couple, the MacFadyens, to cater to their needs.

Kassia had texted Dr Michaelis from London, and told him she was going to take her annual leave after all, then headed north with Damos, on wings of wondrous happiness.

Was she wise to run off with him like this?

Her words to Valerie Cardman echoed in her head, after Valerie had asked her if she'd known Damos long.

'Not very long...'

That first dinner with him on his yacht, for the sake of his funding next season's excavation, then a day out at Blenheim, an evening dining at the Oxford college, and then the Art Deco dinner-dance at the Viscari.

That was all, really. Barely three days.

Yet here she was, plunging into a glorious, wonderful, ecstatic affair with him.

How well do I know him—I mean, really know him?

She heard the question in her head. Heard it and discarded it.

'It's an eagle—I'm sure of it!' Damos exclaimed.

Kassia was glad of the diversion to her thoughts.

'I think eagles keep to the high ground, don't they?' she said doubtfully.

'Well, it's swooped down from the ben, then,' Damos persisted. He lowered his binoculars, turned towards Kassia. 'Why *are* Scottish mountains called bens?' he asked.

'No idea,' said Kassia. 'We must look it up. It's probably Gaelic. I do know what a Munro is, though.'

'A Munro?'

'Yes, they are the mountains that are over three thousand feet—around a thousand metres or so—named after the Victorian mountaineer who first climbed them all. It's now a tradition—to bag a Munro!'

Damos looked interested. 'Could we bag one?'

'We'd need some decent kit,' Kassia said. 'I think there are plenty that don't actually need to be climbed, as such, but even walking would require proper kit. Idiots still go up in trainers and tee shirts, and then slip and fall. And

then the weather turns and Mountain Rescue has to be
called out.'

'We'll buy all the right kit,' Damos pronounced. 'It must
be sold everywhere in Scotland. Then we'll drive to Inverlochry and load up with everything we'll need. Are you up
for it? Bagging a Munro?'

Kassia's eyes rested on him. For Damos she would bag
every Munro he set his sights on. Climbing them with him
at her side would be bliss…

But then everything with Damos at her side was bliss.

'But not today. Today is just a getting-to-know-this-place
day,' he said. He looked around him. 'It really is pretty
good,' he said approvingly. 'A loch all to ourselves…a castle all to ourselves. And sunshine too.'

'And midges. The curse of the Scottish summer!' Kassia
laughed. 'It's better here by the loch, I think. The breeze is
keeping them away.'

'We can have a picnic lunch here,' Damos said.

Kassia groaned. 'How can you think of lunch already,
after that gargantuan breakfast Mrs MacFadyen loaded us
up with? Not so much a full English as a full Scottish. You
put away at least two kippers and half a dozen Scotch pan-
cakes—and that was even before you tackled the bacon and
eggs and toast and marmalade!'

He turned back to her. 'I need to keep my strength up,'
he said.

He dropped a kiss on her mouth. As he drew back, his
eyes were glinting. They were the colour of the dark, peaty
loch water, Kassia thought, as she gazed helplessly back.

'And so do you,' he murmured wickedly. He kissed her
again. 'Glad we came?' he asked.

Her eyes shone as she answered him. 'Oh, yes,' she breathed. 'Oh, yes.'

Her questions—questions she did not even want to ask—evaporated into the clear Highland air. Perhaps she had known Damos only a short while, and perhaps she was being swept away by him, by her own happiness—but how could she argue against it?

And it wasn't just the sensual ecstasy she found in his arms.

That first day with him, after bumping into him like that, out of the blue in Oxford, surely had been a sign? And the easiness between them, when she had never thought there could ever be anything between them—surely that told her there was a connection there? Something that went beyond the heady delights of the nights they spent together?

We can talk together, laugh together, be together. And it feels so right, so natural...as if it were meant to be...

Surely all that was a sign that what was happening between them was good? That she could trust it. Trust Damos—and trust this wonderful, blissful happiness...

'Good,' he said, and there was satisfaction in his voice. Then he pointed towards the end of the little beach. 'There's a path there. Shall we see where it leads? Work up an appetite for lunch?'

He set off, and Kassia followed. The path was wide enough, threading between the shoreline and the spruce and birch, to afford easy going along its mossed surface, even in the trainers she and Damos were wearing. For anything more demanding, let alone bagging a Munro, they would definitely need proper walking boots.

They got them the following morning, after driving into

the local town—a good twelve miles away from their remote castle—together with a fearsome array of mountain-proof gear that Damos insisted on. Kassia smiled indulgently. He was so enthusiastic she hardly liked to point out to him they were unlikely to need quite so much.

The shopkeeper was perfectly happy to cater to his foreign customer's very expensive enthusiasm, and as they finally left, piling umpteen bag-loads into the back of the four-by-four Damos had hired when they'd landed at the airport on arrival, Kassia smiled fondly.

'You,' she said, 'have made that Scotsman a happy, happy man!' Her expression sobered. 'I just wish you hadn't bought so much for me, though, Damos.'

He shut the tailgate with a slam.

'How could I bag a Munro without you? I wouldn't even know what one was, for a start! Now, all that kitting up has made me hungry. Where shall we have lunch? How about over there?'

He pointed across a cobbled square lined with solid granite buildings towards an ancient-looking pub.

They walked towards it together, Kassia slipping her hand into Damos's, knowing how right it felt. How very right it felt to be with him. She felt a glow inside her. However much she might have rushed into this affair with Damos, it was something she was going to trust.

Because I know I can.

Damos's brow furrowed in concentration. Duncan Mac-Fadyen, the husband half of the castle's married couple, was teaching him how to cast a fishing line. It required focus, and just the right amount of flexibility in the wrist.

'Aye, that's right, your grip's fine. Now, lift back, and—'

The line shot forward, arcing across the water. Damos, like his tutor, was standing calf-deep, wearing waders, in the shallow, fast-flowing river.

'Och, not bad…not bad, laddie,' said Duncan MacFadyen. 'Now, reel it in and try again. Watch for those low trees, mind, or they'll tangle your line in a gnat's breath!'

Damos did as he was instructed. His focus was absolute. But then, when his mind was set on something, when he saw a goal he wanted to achieve, he went after it until he had it in his possession—whether it was skill at fly-fishing, or…

His thoughts were diverted for a moment. Behind him, curled up on a groundsheet and tartan rug on the bank, he knew Kassia was sitting, half reading, half watching him, enjoying the pale Scottish sunshine, batting away the midges.

Kassia—her name was sweet in his head. Sweeter than he had ever imagined it would be. But then, how could it not be? She was all that he wanted, and this remote spot in the Highlands was the perfect place for her to be with him. It gave him Kassia all to himself, far away from anyone else. His thoughts were shadowed for a moment. Far away from Greece, where word might get out of their being together. His eyes darkened as he thought of her father and Cosmo Palandrou. Then, deliberately, he pushed them both aside. That whole business was for later—not now.

The shadow left his eyes. Now was for Kassia, for his time with her, for their time together.

And how good it was…how very, very good. Every single moment of every single twenty-four hours.

He felt his breath catch with searing memories. By night, Kassia's passion for him swept him away. She was as ardent in his arms as that very first amazing night. She gave herself so totally to him, so completely—and he returned it in full. Never had he known how it could be…

And by day? Oh, by day there was hour after hour of good times, one after another.

They had bagged their Munro, duly kitted out, making a day of it. They'd chosen an easy one, unused as they both were to hill-walking, ascending up through larch forests to emerge on to the heather and head up to the peak, where they'd hunkered down out of the keening wind to eat their sandwiches and the obligatory Kendal Mint Cake, looking out from their lofty viewpoint over the glories of the Scottish Highlands spread around them, mile after mile.

The next day, needing a rest, they'd set off in the four-by-four to explore the area, driving past brooding lochs and forest-covered slopes, all ringed by heather-covered mountains. They'd stopped for lunch at a wooden lodge, both of them braving haggis and neeps—Damos smiled in recollection—before driving on to seek out a towering waterfall plunging down from the heights, sending myriad rainbows dancing over the spray.

Yesterday Duncan had taken them out on their own loch in a motorboat, exploring the far shore, cruising the length of it, while he regaled them with bloodthirsty tales from Scotland's warlike history, of feuding clans and invasion from both the Vikings and the English. And today Duncan was initiating him into the mysteries of fly-fishing…

'Och, laddie—did I not warn you?'

Duncan MacFadyen's admonishment made Damos realise that he'd let his thoughts wander and his second cast had, indeed, caught the low-hanging branches on the far side of the river. Disentangling it took Damos some time, but he had learnt his lesson and refocussed his attentions. After another half-hour he was doing distinctly better, and Duncan was saying they might try for a fish after lunch.

Lunch was taken seated on folding chairs around a table that opened up from the boot of the four-by-four, which was drawn up near the riverbank for the occasion. As ever, Mrs MacFadyen had done them proud, with a hot raised crust venison pie, poached salmon scallops, root vegetable salad, and fresh-baked crusty bread with salty Scottish butter and tasty Scottish cheese, all washed down with local beer for him and Duncan, and cider for Kassia.

Their repast finished with a 'wee dram' that Duncan produced from the silver hip flask kept about his person.

Damos downed his in one. Kassia choked over hers.

'Oh, good grief!' She looked at Damos and Duncan. 'How on earth do you cope with that?'

Duncan chuckled. 'Practice, lassie, just practice,' he said. He turned to Damos. 'Ye'll be wanting to visit our local distillery, mind. They've a fine single malt—aye, verra fine indeed. Take a bottle or two back with you to Greece. And if it takes your fancy you can buy yourself a cask, keep it here to mature. There's many a rich man does just that.'

Damos's eyes glinted. That might be a good idea. He went into a detailed discussion with Duncan about the excellence of the local whiskies and then, a second and final sampling of Duncan's flask done, went off with him to try his luck with a salmon.

He looked about him as he waded back into the water.

This was good, this day—very, very good. The sun, the scenery, the salmon—and Kassia.

What more could he want right now?

Greece, Athens, Cosmo Palandrou, Yorgos Andrakis and any thought of outmanoeuvring them, helping himself to Cosmo's logistics empire and taking it from under Yorgos Andrakis's nose, seemed very far away.

Irrelevant.

And supremely unimportant.

Kassia's hand hovered over the chess board. She was deeply uncertain over what her next move should be. She could hear the rain pattering on the drawing room's leaded windows. The fine weather had turned, although the MacFadyens had said it was only a summer squall and would blow out overnight. Until it did, the drawing room was a cosy retreat, with the log fire roaring.

They'd kept indoors all day, except for an extremely bracing—and brief—expedition in gumboots and macs to the edge of the loch. Damos had huddled into his waterproofs, but Kassia had laughed, letting the rain wet her hair, and being buffeted by the wind—which had not been cold, only gusty, whipping up the waters of the loch and bowing the birch trees.

Damos, less used to British weather than Kassia, had endured it for five minutes, then called time, heading back to the castle.

She'd gone with him willingly, glancing sideways at him to where raindrops had caught his eyelashes, making her own heart catch as well. As it did every time she looked at him.

She stole another glance at Damos now, still hesitant about her next move. Chess was not her thing. She could never plan or plot ahead sufficiently. Damos—who had, so he'd told her, learnt chess on long sea journeys when he was a deckhand—was way better than her at it.

An enigmatic smile was now playing about his mouth as her fingers hovered indecisively, first over her bishop, and then her knight.

'I wouldn't, you know,' he warned. 'You'll lose your rook if you move your bishop, and you'll expose your queen if you move your knight. Here, this is safest…' He reached to advance one of her unused pawns. 'Now your other bishop can threaten my other rook. Except—'

His hand moved to his own pieces, and before she realised it he'd moved his knight to guard his rook, which then gave his bishop free run at her king.

'Check,' he said.

'Oh, grief—what do I do now?' Kassia said in dismay.

'You move your bishop to intercept mine and protect your king—which will likely lose you your bishop, but…' he pointed out '…it then lets your knight threaten my queen.'

She sat back, pretty much lost. 'I just don't think I've got the right kind of mentality for this,' she confessed. 'I can never see more than one move ahead—if that.'

Damos smiled pityingly. 'Foresight is essential—and planning ahead. And not just in chess, of course. In life, too. It's about spotting unexpected opportunities, if they present themselves,' he went on. 'And then moving to exploit them.'

She frowned. '"Exploit" is not a pleasant word.'

He gave a shrug. 'It just means use,' he said.

'Precisely,' she answered.

He shook his head. 'There's a difference between using opportunities to one's advantage and using people to one's advantage…making use of them.'

'I suppose so,' she allowed.

Her thoughts strayed back to that exchange with him at Blenheim, over the implications of another word—*ambition*. Like 'exploit', and 'use', 'ambition' was another word she was wary of, associating them too much with her father.

But Damos is nothing like him! she retaliated.

He would never make use of other people to his own advantage. Hadn't he told her, that day at Blenheim, that he'd made his money honestly? She should trust that declaration— he would never do anything underhand, exploit others, take advantage of them, use them for his own ends. Her thoughts darkened. Totally unlike her father, who never bothered with people he could not make use of, or who were not useful to him.

She was glad that at that moment there was a knock on the door and then Mrs MacFadyen was coming in, wheeling an old-fashioned wooden tea trolley. Yet again she had done them proud, with fresh bannocks, potato scones, toasted tea cakes and an array of jams and rich butter. If that left any room, there was a plate of crisp shortbread and a freshly baked Dundee cake, glistening with cherries and laden with almonds.

Damos was rubbing his hands in happy anticipation, praising her efforts and thanking Mrs MacFadyen enthusiastically with his ready smile. The stout, middle-aged Scotswoman was no more immune to Damos's charm than any female, and bridled with pleasure at his fulsome compliments.

'Och, get away with you!' she told him, bustling from the room.

Kassia smiled affectionately at Damos. She tried to imagine her father even thanking Mrs MacFadyen, let alone bothering to compliment her.

He and Damos are complete opposites— totally different in character.

She couldn't even make allowances for their differences arising from the origins of their respective wealth. Both men were self-made—her father and Damos—but there the similarities ended. Her father was ruthless, always using other people for his own ends—if he could, he'd have used her, his own daughter. She knew that bitterly well.

Damos is nothing like him—nothing!

It warmed her to think so.

'OK, what is that phrase in English? Are you going to "be mother"?' Damos was asking her.

And, again, it was a welcome interruption of thoughts she did not want to have.

She reached for the teapot—silver and elegant—and filled their cups—fine porcelain. The renting of this castle was not coming cheap, that was for sure. As well as the castle itself, furnished with antiques and luxuriously appointed, there was the lavish fare provided by Mrs Mac-Fadyen, as well as the 'extras' on offer from her husband.

She and Damos had already ticked off fly-fishing and boating on the loch, as well as putting their four-by-four through its offroad paces on a tough, unmade track into the forest. Damos had driven—with Duncan to guide him—

and obviously enjoyed it hugely, while Kassia had hung on for dear life. Duncan had taken them bird watching, too— Damos had been smug about finally spotting a golden eagle soaring way over the mountaintop—and even deer stalking, though both she and Damos had made it clear that they were just going to stalk, not shoot. Kassia was conscious that that was somewhat hypocritical, considering the delicious venison dishes that appeared at the dinner table...

As for dinner—Mrs MacFadyen did them proud there, too, every night, and Damos and Kassia responded accordingly. Though they dressed down for their activities in the day—their newly bought walking kit was seeing a lot of use—at night Kassia delighted in dressing the part for Damos. He put on his tux, and she the pale blue chiffon evening gown he'd insisted on buying her in London— along with an array of well-cut co-ordinates that flattered, rather than concealed, her tall figure.

Now, with the wonderful new confidence in herself that Damos had released in her, she knew that for the first time in her life she could really enjoy wearing fashionable clothes, making the most of herself instead of the least. And to that end, every night here in the Highlands, she made up her face for the evening and dressed her hair elegantly, glowing inside as Damos's admiring eyes rested on her.

Then she would take his gallantly proffered arm and walk down the imposing flight of stairs beside him, sweeping into the drawing room for pre-dinner drinks and then taking their places at either end of the polished oak table in the adjacent dining room, laden with silver and crystal, shimmering in the candlelight. There, they would await the arrival not of dinner, but of the piper who would announce it. He was Duncan's nephew, and he would march into the dining room in full Highland regalia, the music of the pibroch filling the room.

After he'd retired, dinner would follow hard on his heels. With vintage wines, rich dishes and traditional Scottish desserts, they dined sumptuously—Kassia had swiftly become a fan of Scottish raspberries, heather honey, toasted oatmeal and whisky cream whipped up into cranachan.

And finally, after heading back upstairs, her hand once more on Damos's arm, she would be escorted to their bedchamber. And there, with a sensuous skill that sent her into helpless meltdown every time, he would let his fingertips glide over her skin, arousing, touch by touch, all the sweet, sweet fire that he always so wondrously elicited from her and set glowing in every tremulous cell of her body.

To make her his.

Consummately, consumingly his...

And he is mine—oh, he is mine.

Because he was. Surely he was? How could it be otherwise when every night she held him as close to her as he held her to him? His heart beat against hers; hers beat against his. As if it could never be any different.

And in those precious hours—in the sweet, slow watches of the night—how could she not think, hope, believe what every passing day, every passionate night, was telling her.

I am falling in love with him.

Was it wise to let it happen? To give herself up to all that she was feeling? To give herself up to the tremulous, uncertain, but oh-so-longed-for hope that Damos might be falling in love as well? Did she...could she...dare to hope...?

CHAPTER NINE

DAMOS FROWNED. Kassia was having her morning shower—he could hear the water splashing—and he was using the time to catch up with his business affairs. Athens was two hours ahead of the UK, and the morning there was well advanced. Most of the updates he was receiving were routine, but the one that was currently bringing a frown to his forehead was not.

Things were on the move between Cosmo Palandrou and Yorgos Andrakis, so his sources were telling him. The director of a well-known firm of corporate accountants who specialised in mergers and acquisitions, and were known to have been previously engaged by Andrakis on such matters, had been seen arriving with his team at Cosmo's company HQ. Andrakis was clearly having due diligence done.

And there was more. Andrakis had been reported as lunching with the senior partner of a law firm specialising in inheritance and marital contract law, giving weight to what Damos was sure Andrakis had in mind for Cosmo and his daughter.

Damos closed down his laptop, still frowning. But not because it was clear that Andrakis was moving in on Cosmo Palandrou. Because two worlds were colliding.

The world of Kassia, here with him in this idyllic Highland retreat, so wonderful to him, so special, theirs and theirs alone.

And the world of his life in Athens—his business life, that had driven him all his life.

He set the laptop aside, getting to his feet and walking over to the bedroom window, with its breathtaking view out over the loch and the forest and mountains beyond. The fortnight with Kassia was flashing by...day after glorious day, night after passionate night.

I don't want it to end.

The assertion was in his head, almost audible and crystal-clear. He heard it again, more clearly still.

His gaze rested on the vista beyond, his thoughts running.

His time here in the Highlands must end.

But not my time with Kassia.

The words were as clear as the Highland air around him. And their imperative just as clear.

There is no reason for it to end.

Why should it? Why should his time with Kassia not continue when they were back in Greece? Oh, once—long ago now, it seemed—he had assumed that the affair he was going to engineer with her would end once its purpose had been achieved. But now...

Now it was absurd to think that.

He felt his mouth tighten, made himself think of what he'd just read about Andrakis and Cosmo Palandrou. For an instant he wished it all to perdition—wished he knew nothing about it, knew nothing of what they were planning and scheming. He consigned his own whole damn plan to perdition as well. He wanted nothing to do with it any more—nothing to do with his plan for getting hold of Cosmo's empire.

Then he drew in a breath—a sharp one. Forced his brain back into the gear it normally operated in, the well-oiled channels it was used to. Acquiring Cosmo's logistics business made perfect sense. It would provide an expansion and a synergy for him that would significantly increase his own reach, bringing in handsome profits after he'd knocked the ailing business into shape and had it properly managed.

That hadn't changed.

His mouth tightened. And nor had the fact that Andrakis was going to try and use his own daughter to get hold of it first.

Unless…

Unless I spike his guns.

Using the method he'd envisaged from the first.

It's all I have to do.

That was the beauty of it—the simplicity.

A question forced its way into his head. He didn't want it to, but it did all the same.

And is it still that simple?

He felt his jaw tighten, his eyes resting on the surface of the loch, its waters dark and impenetrable. Just as were his thoughts.

He brought them to the surface. Saw them clearly.

Yes. Yes, it was still that simple. All he had to do was show Cosmo that Andrakis's daughter was not available to be his bride—just as he had planned from the off.

It really is that simple.

And because it was so simple there was no reason not to stick to it—not to go ahead with it…go through with it.

For a moment longer his gaze went on resting on the dark waters below, as if there were currents moving deep below the surface that had not previously been there, stirring deep waters in unknown ways.

Then, abruptly, he turned away, not wanting to think about it any longer. The day stretched ahead, and they were planning on heading off further afield, doing more sightseeing—this time towards the coast and Dunrobin Castle—for the day was fine and sunny.

He could hear that the shower had cut out, and shortly afterwards Kassia was stepping into the bedroom, wrapped in a towel, her hair pinned up loosely on her head, tendrils falling damply around her face. She looked effortlessly beautiful—bare shoulders, long legs, slender body.

He crossed to her, with a familiar glint in his eyes and an even more familiar tightening in his loins.

'That,' he told her, and he could hear the husk in his own voice, 'is a very dangerous thing to do, Kassia. If you want us to set off sightseeing in good time.'

His hand reached for where she'd knotted the towel over her breasts, gently easing the knot loose.

She caught his hands. 'Damos, no!' she laughed.

His eyebrows rose. 'No?'

'Yes! As in no,' she said firmly, stepping away from him. 'Breakfast will be waiting for us!'

He gave her a considering look. 'Hmm, tough choice… One of Mrs MacFadyen's gargantuan breakfasts versus making passionate love to you.'

She laughed again. He liked to hear the sound, and answered it with a laugh of his own.

'OK, breakfast wins. But…' he held up a hand '…don't think I won't claim making passionate love to you when we get back this afternoon!'

She blew him a kiss, but kept her distance.

Damos knew why—and knew, with a sense of deeply masculine satisfaction, that she would have been just as happy to defer breakfast a while…

'It's a date,' she promised, and her eyes had a glint in them that matched his own.

She turned away, fetching fresh undies from the chest of drawers and a smart pair of trousers—nothing baggy any more, Damos thought with satisfaction—and a stylish cotton top to go with them that skimmed her breasts and shaped her slender waist. Brushing her hair out, she clipped it back with a barrette. Its new rich colour still held, catching the sunlight.

He watched as she applied a little mascara, a trace of lip gloss, but nothing more. There was appreciation in his regard. Oh, when she went for the full works—face, hair and gown—she could look sensational, just as he'd told her that evening at the Viscari Art Deco dinner-dance.

But she does not need to—not for me. Just to see her like, this is enough…more than enough.

Just being with her was more than enough.

And he had no intention—none—that he should not be with her…

OK, so their time here in the Highlands was coming to an end and soon they would be returning to Greece. But there…

I'll get the business of Cosmo and her father out of the way, dispose of it, and then focus entirely on Kassia.

It was a pleasing prospect—a very pleasing one indeed.

Kassia and me—me and Kassia...

Again, as he had that very first night with her in London, he felt the strange, powerful emotion sweeping up in him that he could not identify. He only knew that it was possessing him.

Body and soul...

'Well, it was certainly a magnificent place,' Kassia said, as they headed back to their very own castle—a mere scrap in comparison with the vastness of Dunrobin Castle, another ducal residence, this time of the Duke of Sutherland. 'Such a pity about the Highland Clearances, though.' She gave a sigh. 'So ruthless...'

Damos steered the four-by-four along a road threading through dramatic scenery. 'Sheep were simply more profitable than crofting,' he said.

'So that makes it all right? Evicting the crofters? Burning down their crofts so they couldn't return?'

He shook his head. 'It's understandable, Kassia. The profit motive is a powerful one. It drives people to do things they might otherwise regret.'

She felt unease prick at her.

But there are some actions that shouldn't ever be undertaken. However profitable! However much money is at stake.

Her thoughts darkened. Her father would have no qualms about doing whatever was necessary to make a profit. Whatever it did to anyone else. Her expression softened again. But Damos was not like that at all. He'd just been stating blunt truths—not advocating them. Let alone practising them.

He was speaking again.

'And don't forget, as we learnt today, that crofting life was hard for the crofters. The idea was that they should move to towns, get other jobs—easier ones—or even emigrate, as so many did, and make a better life for themselves in the colonies. It wasn't completely black and white.' His voice changed. 'It seldom is,' he said.

She could hear something in his voice—a note of constraint—and looked across at him as he drove back towards their castle along the winding road. Some things *were* black and white, though, surely...?

As if he sensed her doubts over what he was saying, he turned towards her. A smile lightened his face.

'Let's not talk about such sad things,' he said. 'They are over and done with, thankfully. Let's talk about us, Kassia.'

His smile deepened, but then he had to flick his eyes back to the road again, as they climbed up towards a col. For all the warmth of his smile, Kassia felt a chill. Their fortnight was nearly up—what would come after?

Is this all there will ever be?

It was the question she did not want to ask...and yet the closer they came to the end of their holiday, the more intrusive it had become.

She knew the answer she wanted to give—longing filled her, and hope—but would it be the same for Damos? She had dared to hope...but hopes could be dashed. Discarded and dismissed.

Damos was about to speak again, still keeping his eyes

on the road, his hands on the steering wheel. There seemed to be a lump forming in her throat...a stone... The dread of what he was going to say.

'I know I'm based in Athens, and you're not, but I think we'll be able to manage, won't we? For weekends together, at least?' he posed. 'And we can grab all the holiday time we can get together as well?'

The stony lump in her throat dissolved instantly as relief coursed through her—his words were music to her ears.

'Oh, I'm sure we can!' she exclaimed.

He reached towards her with one hand, flashing his warm smile at her, then looked back to the road again.

'Great—so that's sorted. Now, how do we make the most of our last day here tomorrow? What about a visit to the whisky distillery Duncan recommended?'

'Good idea,' she agreed.

Warmth was filling her, as if several wee drams had just been consumed, making her glow from the inside. This time in the Highlands was *not* to be the end for her and Damos!

He still wants me—wants us to be together. How wonderful is that?

Again, she knew the answer. It was more wonderful than she dared believe...

To keep him in my life...and me in his...

'We can get a couple of bottles for the MacFadyens,' Damos was saying now. 'As a thank-you to them.'

'And maybe I can buy a scarf or a brooch for Mrs Mac-Fadyen,' Kassia said.

Happiness at what Damos had said to her about them seeing each other in Greece was filling her.

They were descending now, towards the valley in which their own loch lay. Soon Damos swung into the driveway of their castle. As he did so, Kassia heard her phone beeping from her handbag. She reached down to fetch it out, but as she glanced to see who the message was from her happiness collapsed like a punctured balloon.

It was from her father.

Summoning her to Athens.

Damos stood by the edge of the loch, its dark water lapping near his feet. Kassia stood nearby, hands plunged into her jacket pocket, her face grave. He stooped to pick up a pebble, flat and thin, and stood up to skim it across the loch. The late sun, still high at this latitude at this season, despite the hour, had gone behind a cloud.

'You don't have to go,' he said.

He didn't look at Kassia. But he could tell from her tone of voice that she was troubled.

'I think I do, Damos. He isn't asking much—just that I show up for some dinner or other. You know that he does that from time to time. I turn up and be his docile daughter, and then he goes on being patron of the museum. It's… it's worked so far. And I suppose, in a way, I don't want to break with him entirely. I just wish, sometimes, that he—'

She broke off, then spoke again.

'That he wasn't always so dismissive of me. I know I disapprove of so much about him…how ruthless he is in business…but, well…' She swallowed. 'He's still my father, and it would be nice if sometimes…just sometimes… he might think something good of me.'

'Do you?'

He looked at her now. Her face was troubled. But then his thoughts were troubled too. He knew the reason for Andrakis's summons to his daughter. He was going to parade her in front of Cosmo, present her as a suitable bride, and set his scheme in motion.

But that was never going to happen.

Cosmo himself would to reject it out of hand.

The moment he knows what is between Kassia and myself.

On the short walk from the car down to the loch's edge thoughts had been marching through Damos's head. Now that the moment had come—now that Andrakis had shown his hand, made his move, set the timetable—Damos knew he had to react just as he'd always planned to do.

But do I have to do it in that way?

That was the question incising in his head now. What if he and Kassia simply flew back to Athens and went out and about together? Let word get out that they were an item? The trouble was, time was tight. Kassia had relayed, with reluctance in her voice—both at the summons itself and the high-handed short notice afforded her—that her father had demanded her presence the evening after tomorrow. The very day they were leaving the Highlands. And he had told her to present herself at, of all places, the Viscari Athena.

The irony was not lost on Damos.

The venue itself was a giveaway. It was newly opened, to great fanfare, and tables at the rooftop gourmet restaurant were like gold dust. Andrakis was clearly wanting to impress Cosmo.

Thoughts churned in his head. Unless Kassia refused the summons—and she seemed to be disinclined to do so, as she'd just said—there wouldn't be time for word to get out that he and Kassia were a couple. Which left only—

Only the way I originally envisaged.

And besides…

His question to her just now echoed in his head. Kassia's father had always sneered at his own daughter, castigating her cruelly for what he considered her lack of looks, condemning her to think so little of herself.

But now that is all changed!

No one—not even her cold-hearted father—could dismiss her now. Not any longer.

Kassia was speaking, answering his question. There was a sad, plaintive quality to her voice.

'But he never will, I know,' she was saying.

Damos's expression changed. Decisiveness fired in him.

He met Kassia's eyes full on. 'Oh, yes, he will,' he said, and there was something in his voice that only he himself could hear.

He stooped, picked up another flat pebble, straightened, and hurled it out across the loch. Then he took Kassia's hand.

'He will,' he said again.

CHAPTER TEN

KASSIA'S NERVES WERE stretched to breaking point. Oh, could she really go through with this? Inside she was trembling like a jelly. She had never enjoyed the times when her father summoned her, but she'd learnt to get through them with minimum stress. Simply by staying quiet and meek and docile, as she'd told Damos. By being as inconspicuous as possible.

But tonight…

Tonight was going to be totally different.

She felt her nerves jangle again as they made their way into the palatial lobby of the Viscari Athena. Given their early-evening arrival from the UK that day, Damos had booked them into a hotel that served the airport, to give Kassia the maximum time possible to get ready for the evening ahead. Even so, it had been a rush.

She'd had to shower, wash her hair, and then a hairstylist and beautician had arrived—Damos had seen to it—to style her hair, make up her face, do her nails, and then help her into the close-fitting bias-cut silvery dress she'd worn at the Viscari St James that unforgettable evening.

When she was finally ready, Damos's eyes had lit up.

'Sensational…' he breathed. 'Just sensational.' He came

forward to take her hands, press them in his. 'Your father is going to be *stunned*!' He raised each hand to his lips in turn, then lowered them, holding them warmly still. 'Never, *never* again will he be able to say the slightest derisive thing about your looks! Every head will turn when they see you!'

They were turning now, Kassia could tell as, nerves pinched yet again, they crossed the foyer heading to the elevators. If it hadn't been for Damos at her side, and her hand clutching the sleeve of his tuxedo, she would have cut and run. Not that running in these four-inch heels was possible…

But I won't run—I won't!

Resolve lifted her chin. All her adult life her father had disparaged her and belittled her for being plain and un-lovely. Tonight she would show him.

It had been Damos's idea, out by the loch.

'It's the perfect opportunity to show him how fantastic you can look!'

And she did look fantastic—she knew she did. Her fa-ther would have to acknowledge it. It would be impossible for him to deny it. All the same, she knew that even with her new confidence about her looks she wouldn't have had the courage to look this incredibly glamorous for her father without Damos at her side.

As they stepped into the elevator she glanced at him, expecting to see a reassuring smile on his face for her. But he was looking ahead, not at her, and there seemed to be a tension across his shoulders. She wondered why…

Surely, she thought, he could not be apprehensive about turning up with her this evening? Whatever the reason her father wanted her to dine with him tonight, whoever he was entertaining, what did it matter if Damos was with her? They were a couple now—and it was something her father would have to accept.

Damos had said as much.

'If your father is happy with my joining the party, then fine—but if not... Well, there's no reason we need stay,' he had told her. *'We'll have dinner together, by ourselves, and then why don't we hit a nightspot? I can't wait to start showing you off.'* His voice had been warm. *'I want all of Athens to see you with me!'*

The elevator was slowing, gliding to a halt. The doors were opening.

And now Damos did look at her. With her heels she was almost at his eye level, but not quite. Was it that slight angle that suddenly seemed to make his eyes look veiled... unreadable?

Then her nerves pinched again, and she tightened her grip on his sleeve.

He patted her hand briefly. 'You can do this,' he said, nodding at her.

She drew a breath, nodding wordlessly in reply and wondering, as they stepped out into the restaurant lobby, whether she had just imagined that she had heard him murmur, low and almost inaudibly, 'So can I...'

Damos led her forward. His shoulders were as tense as steel. Doubt knifed through him, but he thrust it aside. No time for that now. Whatever questions he'd put to himself about what he was doing had been set aside.

Out by the loch, with Kassia telling him of her father's summons, she had given him an opening he'd realised he could use. So she longed for her father not to deride her appearance as he habitually did? Well, tonight would be her chance. She would look as sensational at the Viscari Athena as she had at the Viscari St James.

And it's what I want too.

It would play perfectly to his own agenda. With Kassia looking such a knockout there could be no mistaking his interest in her—his involvement with her. And Yorgos Andrakis and Cosmo Palandrou would not mistake it either...

On his sleeve, he felt Kassia's fingers tighten. Well, there was no need. This would not take long. Oh, he'd told her that he'd be happy to join her father's party, if invited— but that was not going to happen. His presence would most definitely not be welcome, he thought grimly.

No, he would be whisking Kassia away the moment Cosmo and Yorgos got the message. He'd made a reservation for himself and her, requesting a table far away from Yorgos Andrakis. As far as anyone else would see, he and Kassia would simply be greeting her father and his guest, then dining *à deux* on their own. Reinforcing to all who saw them the fact that he and Kassia were together.

He paused by the desk, giving his name, and telling the clerk that they would be meeting with Kyrios Andrakis first. Then, with Kassia on his arm, he walked into the restaurant, raking his eyes over the tables, looking for her father.

He saw him immediately.

His mouth tightened. Yorgos had only one dinner guest with him.

Cosmo Palandrou.

Damos's eyes hardened. As they headed towards them he could see heads turning—Kassia, looking as sensational as she was, was drawing all eyes. But there were only two pairs of eyes he wanted to see her.

And see her they were…

He saw it happen. Saw her father, deep in conference with his dinner guest—his *only* dinner guest—glance up. Saw his eyes focus on who had just come into the restaurant. Saw, for a moment, complete blankness in them, as if he had no idea who the woman walking towards him was. Then, as they approached, the blankness changed to incredulous recognition.

In one slow-motion movement, his incredulous gaze took in Damos, at Kassia's side. And his recognition changed to something else…a different expression taking hold of his face.

They reached his table, and Damos could feel Kassia's hand gripping his sleeve. But right now he had no spare attention for her. No attention for anything except what was happening.

Tension speared through him. So much was at stake.

And yet…

I want this done. Over and done with. So I can get the hell out of here with Kassia. I want Andrakis and Cosmo to get the message I am sending them, and for Andrakis to know his plan is now impossible. That I have made it so, and that now Cosmo will be looking elsewhere for a bride. And for a buyer…

It would not take him long to achieve all that—it was happening right now…

Cosmo Palandrou had looked up too.

Damos's eyes went from Yorgos to him. Then back to Yorgos. Then he smiled.

It was a smile, he knew, of victory.

Checkmate.

It was a sweet, sweet moment.

Kassia's grip on Damos's sleeve was rigid. Her father was staring at her as though he could not believe what he was seeing. Kassia could understand why.

Her eyes flickered for a moment, taking in the man dining with her father. Dim recognition plucked at her. It was Cosmo Palandrou. She'd met him before, at a larger dinner party a year or more ago, when her father had summoned her there. She took in the fact that the table was only set for three—which seemed odd. What was so special about Cosmo Palandrou that he was her father's only guest? And why would her father want her here as well?

She hadn't liked Cosmo Palandrou the first time she'd met him—he'd been as dismissive of her as her father always was, and he was physically repellent—overweight, with heavy jowls and small, pouchy eyes. His manner had been rude and abrupt, and she knew his company had often been in the press over a number of strikes and industrial disputes, as well as breaking environmental standards.

But she had no attention to give him now—all her focus was on her father. A tremor of trepidation went through her, and the sudden cowardly wish that she'd simply worn the unflattering green dress she'd bought in England and done nothing to her face and hair. Then she rallied. This was her golden chance to show her father that she was no longer the Plain Jane daughter he'd always castigated her for being. Maybe even finally to win his approval…

A stab of longing went through her, which she knew

she should not allow. She had long ago given up on doing something right by his endlessly critical and dismissive standards…

But surely tonight there would be something different from the offhand way he usually noted her arrival? Surely this time he couldn't help but react differently, given her stunningly altered appearance?

But he was still staring at her—just staring—so she decided to make an attempt to break the moment, to give him some kind of greeting.

She never got the chance. Abruptly, her father was thrusting himself to his feet, his bulk considerable. Colour was riding up in his cheeks, his face working. Alarm speared in Kassia as she saw her father's beefy hands fist on the table.

Then words spat from him. Words that made her blench. Crude and explicit.

But they were not directed at her.

It was Damos who got them—full in his face.

Kassia's head shot round, She was appalled at what her father had hurled at Damos.

But Damos's mouth had merely tightened, his features steeled. There was a sudden hollowing in her stomach. He looked like a stranger to her. His face hard, his eyes harder.

Then Cosmo Palandrou was lurching to his feet as well, his expression ugly. He twisted his head, ignoring both Damos and herself. His focus was entirely on her father, and he was glaring at him with malevolence—a fury that contorted his ill-favoured features.

'What the hell are you playing at, Andrakis?' The question was a hiss, like a venomous snake.

She heard Damos's voice. Cutting across him like a knife. Answering him.

'Cool it—Andrakis is playing at nothing.' His voice was dismissive.

Cosmo's eyes flashed back across the table to Damos. He opened his mouth to speak, but Damos cut in again. His expression was still steeled, and there was a glint in his eyes too, a hardness in their depths.

His mouth twisted, and his voice changed as he spoke again. There was open mockery in it now. 'Relax. Andra-kis's deal will still be on the table, Cosmo—if you still want to pick it up now, of course.' He paused, holding the other man's glaring gaze. '*Do* you?' he asked. It was a taunt—open and derisive.

Cosmo Palandrou surged forward across the table, rage in his face, mouthing expletives.

A cry broke from Kassia. What was happening? Dear God, what was happening? Nothing made sense—nothing at all.

Then her father was speaking. More than speaking. He was all but yelling, his features livid. And now it was not directed at Damos. It was coming at her. Right at her. Ugly and vile.

'Slut! You shameless, whoring slut!'

She gave another cry, horror and disbelief ravening across her face.

Her father's fisted hands slammed down on the table-cloth. '*Thee mou! Cristos!* How stupid can you be? Letting yourself be used by this…this…'

He used another word that made Kassia cry out again. But her father was storming on, his face filled with fury.

'He's used you—and you're too cretinously stupid to see it!'

'Enough!' Damos's voice was like a blade, slashing down. 'You will not speak to her like that!'

Her father's fury turned on him. 'I will speak to my *whore* of a daughter any way I want! The whore *you've* made of her!'

His lashing fury moved back to Kassia, his face enraged and twisting.

'You stupid, gullible, brainless idiot! You stand there, looking like the tart he's made of you… But do you really think that Damos Kallinikos would have looked twice at you if you hadn't been my daughter?' His scorn lashed at her. 'He wouldn't have given you the time of day, let alone warmed his bed with you! He's used you—made a whore of you—to get at me. Just to get at me! Attack me! Do you understand that? You imbecilic, whoring slut—'

She broke away from him, stumbling. A nightmare was enveloping her. She saw glass doors, staggered towards them blindly, hearing voices, harsh and ugly and raging, behind her. Her father's, Cosmo's—and Damos's too. Slicing through the air.

She had to silence them.

But they could not be silenced. How could they?

She reached the glass doors, pushed them open, plunged forward. She was out on some kind of paved terrace, set with tables. There were a few diners only, for the evening had turned chilly. The roof garden stretched beyond, framing the distant Parthenon, illuminated as it always was by night.

A path to the right opened up between high bushes and

she stumbled along it, her ankles turning in her high heels. There was a voice behind her—urgent, calling her name. She reached a little clearing set with benches and lit with ornamental lanterns. Several more paths opened up. She paused, catching her broken breath, desperate still to get away…just get away…

'Kassia!'

Damos strode up to her. In the dim light his face looked stark. Like a stranger's.

But he *was* a stranger—a complete stranger—someone she had never known…

Till now. Till this nightmare.

He tried to reach for her arm, but she jerked away.

'Get away from me!'

His eyes flared. 'Kassia—I have to speak to you.'

'Get away from me!' she cried again.

She tried to plunge forward again, down a path—any path. Any path that would take her away from this nightmare. But she felt her arm taken in a grip she could not shake.

'Kassia, listen—*listen*!'

'To what? What else is there for me to hear? My father has said it all!'

Damos swore. Vehement and vicious.

'Your father is a brute! Don't take any notice of him— he isn't worth it!'

She rounded on him. 'And you? Are you worth anything more? *Are* you? Because what the hell was going on in there? What is all this *about*? Why is Cosmo Palandrou here? Why did you say my father's deal would still be on the table for him if he wanted it? What deal? And why…

why did my father say those things about me? Those hideous, hideous things!'

The words, the questions, tumbled from her, anguished and uncomprehending. She was caught in this nightmare. She'd been catapulted into it. Her heart was pounding—she could feel it—and there was nausea inside her, rising up. She stared at Damos, still hearing her father's vile denunciation ringing in her ears.

Desperate denial filled her.

It's not true, it's not true!

'Damos, *why*?' she cried again.

Her eyes clung to his, but there was something wrong about them…something wrong in his face, in its starkness, in the tightness of his mouth, the set of his jaw.

A sudden fear went through her.

Damos was speaking, answering her. His voice was as tight as his expression.

'There is no good way to tell you this, Kassia—and I wish to God you'd never had to know! I never intended you to. But Cosmo Palandrou was there tonight because your father wants you to marry him,' Damos bit out, his face stark and grim. He gave a harsh, short laugh, bereft of humour, and his breath incised sharply. 'Make that *wanted* you to marry him.'

Kassia was staring at Damos. There was still something wrong with his face—but then there was something wrong with the universe right now. Something hideously wrong…

'Marry Cosmo?' she said. Her voice was hollow, her eyes uncomprehending.

'Yes,' Damos said grimly. 'Look, I have to explain…'

She heard him incise his breath again, as if forcing

himself to speak, and when he did constraint tightened every word.

'Your father is after Cosmo's company. Cosmo's playing hardball and holding out for more. So...' His breath knifed again. 'Your father was going to throw you into play. Offer Cosmo the role of his son-in-law.' His voice changed. 'Kassia, I'm sorry. I'm so sorry that he said such things to you! I never—'

She raised her hand to stop him. What Damos had just told her about Cosmo Palandrou could not be true! It couldn't be! Her father couldn't possibly want what Damos said. And yet...

Why else would Cosmo Palandrou be here this evening?

The hollow inside her became suddenly a yawning chasm, And why else had her father been so angry to see her with Damos? So angry with Damos?

'He called me those vile things because you were with me,' she said blankly. 'But why?' Her words were suddenly as heavy as stones. 'Why was he saying...saying that you... you were only interested in me because I'm his daughter? And why was he so angry with *you*...?'

Damos's face was stark, his features like granite. She saw him take a breath—brief and harsh.

'Because,' he said tightly, his mouth set—as if, she thought suddenly, he did not want to speak but was making himself do so, 'your father is not the only party interested in acquiring Cosmo Palandrou's company.'

Kassia heard his words. And as she did so a wheel started to turn very slowly somewhere in the recesses of her shattered mind.

'You,' she said. Her voice was empty.

He nodded. There was still that closed expression on his face, the same tightness in his voice and in the set of his mouth.

'Yes. I intend to acquire Cosmo's freight and logistics business,' he said. 'So I don't want him selling to your father—'

She cut across him. 'You knew Cosmo Palandrou would be here this evening, didn't you?' Her voice was still empty. 'You wanted to turn up with me—*didn't you*? So that he would see us together. So my father would see us…see us and know—' She broke off.

That same closed, stark look was in Damos's face.

'Yes,' he said. His hand tightened on her arm. 'Kassia, all I wanted was for your father and Cosmo to know about us. Then your father's scheme would collapse on the spot and we could just walk away. I never thought your father would react like that! Would say such things to his own daughter!'

The vile words her father had thrown at her were still slicing through her, each one drawing blood.

'My father does not take opposition well,' she heard herself say, her tone expressionless. 'And his temper,' she said, 'is very short.'

But that wheel in her head was still moving forward, slowly and agonisingly. Taking her to a place she did not want to go. A place she would have given all she possessed not to be taken to. But those words that her father had hurled at her, so vile and ugly, were taking her there.

She heard them again now, incising across her consciousness as if with sharpest knife.

'Do you really think Damos Kallinikos would have

*looked twice at you if you hadn't been my daughter? He's
used you—'*

Carefully, very carefully, she lifted Damos's hand off
her arm and took a step back. The air felt thick, like the
toxic air of a distant planet. The planet that she was now
on. A million light years from all she had known. Had
thought she knew…

'Tell me something,' she said, and she thought there was
something wrong with her voice, as well as with the air she
was breathing. It was starting to suffocate her. 'When did
decide you wanted Cosmo's company? And when did you
learn of my father's charming plans for me?' She stopped,
trying to take another breath, but the toxic air was in her
throat now, and it was suffocating her.

She forced herself on. Forced herself to ask the final
question. The question she would have given everything
not to ask, but must. *Must*…

'Was it before you showed up at the dig?'

He did not answer. His face had closed.

She let her eyes rest on him. On Damos. On the man
who was not Damos. Not the man she'd just spent the three
most wonderful weeks of her life with. Three weeks which
had transformed her life. Transformed *her*…

Into a fool…a gullible, cretinous idiot.

Her father's vicious, excoriating, scathing castigation
rang pitilessly in her ears. And more words too.

'Whore! Slut—shameless slut!'

She wanted to silence them, but it was impossible…
impossible. Oh, dear God. To think she had wanted her
father to see that she was no longer the crushed, dowdy
daughter he'd always condemned her as being! To think

that she'd thought her glamorous new look would achieve that…her fabulous transformation into a woman that any man might desire…

That Damos might desire.

A cry rose up in her from very deep, excoriating her.

Fool—oh, fool! It was never about you—never. Not for a single moment! It was only about—

'You knew,' she said, never taking her eyes from him though each word was like a scalpel on her skin. 'You knew that Cosmo Palandrou would not want to…to marry me if I had already—' She swallowed, and it was as if that scalpel was peeling the skin from inside her throat. 'If I had already, as my father so succinctly put it, *"warmed your bed…"*'

She fell silent. What else was there to say? What else could ever be said?

Except the word that fell from Damos's lips now.

'Yes,' he said.

She turned away.

She felt her arm seized, heard words breaking from Damos.

'Kassia—listen…listen to me! *Please!* It wasn't…isn't…'

She gave another cry, yanking her arm free, plunging down a path on feet that were stumbling, desperate.

Desperate to get away. Away from Damos.

For ever.

Damos watched her go. The universe seemed to have moved into another reality. One he didn't recognise. He had not given consent to it…given it permission to exist.

He turned. Headed back into the restaurant. He was

conscious, with a fragment of his mind, that he was being looked at—the ugly scene at Andrakis's table had not gone unnoticed, unheard... The table was deserted now, and he could see the *maître d'* hurrying up to him, his expression anxious.

'Cancel my reservation,' Damos said, and walked past him, back out into the lobby beyond. Heading for the elevator.

He needed to find Kassia. Needed to find her, talk to her, explain to her.

It isn't the way she thinks it is! The way her thug of a father is making her think it is!

He felt his hands clench as he strode into the elevator. Hell, hell and hell! He should have realised that Andrakis would explode as he had. Take his fury at Damos out on his daughter.

He punched the button for the lobby and the lift hurtled down. Urgency filled him. Kassia might have come down in a service lift, but he could surely catch her as she left the hotel. He would wait by the entrance. If he missed her there, he'd find her at their hotel. But find her he must—he *must*.

How had he so misjudged the situation? Exposed Kassia like that? Self-castigation whipped through him.

The elevator doors sliced open, and he plunged out into the lobby.

He heard a snarl behind him. With a fraction of a second to spare, he whirled around.

Yorgos Andrakis was lurching up to him, coming out of the cocktail bar opening off the lobby.

'Looking for my *whore* of a daughter? She won't touch

you—even though being your whore is all she's good for now!'

Yorgos Andrakis's face was ugly with fury and venom. Damos wanted to make it uglier still. His fisted hand moved faster than his thoughts. He smashed it into Yorgos Andrakis's face, his own face contorting, and then grabbed the man by his lapels, hauling him towards him.

'Don't *ever* call her that.'

His voice was a low, deadly blade, thrusting right into Yorgos's face. He drew back his fisted hand, ready to strike again. To pulverise. Smash to pieces.

He never made contact.

Kassia collapsed into the back of the taxi she'd flagged down when she'd emerged at the back of the hotel via the service staircase. Faintly, she gave the driver the name of the hotel near the airport and he set off. She closed her eyes, her face twisting painfully. She gave a smothered cry that was almost a sob, but she stifled it. She must not break down. Not now. Not yet.

At the hotel she made it to their room, terrified that she would find Damos there. But it was empty. She tore herself out of her gown, threw on some clothes to travel in, grabbed her handbag with her passport and credit cards.

Speed was essential—Damos could burst in at any point.

She made it downstairs, out of the hotel, and threw herself into the hotel shuttle bus. Minutes later she was in Departures, her eyes desperately scanning the board for a flight that had not yet closed. She didn't care where she went. Just away from this nightmare.

But she knew, with agony inside her, as she finally collapsed into her last-minute seat on a flight to Amsterdam, that she was taking the nightmare with her...

Damos emerged from the police station unshaven, his tuxedo crumpled, into the cold light of dawn. Both he and Yorgos Andrakis had been arrested after hotel security had rushed over, separating the two men, hustling them both out on to the pavement, then summoning the police. What had happened to Kassia's father he neither knew nor cared—he himself had been discharged with a caution.

The reason for his violent outburst at Yorgos Andrakis had been sympathetically regarded, hence his discharge. But for his night at the police station his phone had been removed from him. Now it had been restored to him he was phoning urgently, hailing a taxi to throw himself into, heading back to their hotel.

Heading back to Kassia.

Urgency drove him. Urgency and so much more.

But it drove him in vain.

His number had been blocked by her.

She had left the hotel.

There was no trace of her.

Over the following days there was no trace of her at her workplace either—and Dr Michaelis had been reserved in the extreme when Damos had finally badgered someone sufficiently to get him to speak to him directly. He had informed him, stiltedly, that Kassia had taken indefinite leave.

Damos's next attempt had been at her mother's house. The housekeeper there had been equally reserved. No, her employer's daughter was not there. She had no knowledge of her whereabouts, and she could not give out any information on where her mother was at the moment. She believed she was no longer in Spain, but would not take it upon herself to say when she might be returning to the UK.

Frustration bit through Damos.

More than frustration. Worse.

Desperation.

CHAPTER ELEVEN

Kassia lay on the yacht's sun deck under an awning. Her eyes were shut, but she was not sleeping. Thoughts, bitter and toxic, were circling in her head.

I deserve what my father threw at me—I deserve it!

She had been as cretinously stupid as he'd said.

Thinking it was me Damos was interested in.

There had been only one thing he'd wanted—and it wasn't her.

Acid tears seeped beneath her eyelids. To think she had thought it mere chance, a coincidence, that she had bumped into Damos like that in Oxford...

Oh, fool to think that!

He planned it from the start—planned it all. Right from visiting the excavation. All that stuff about wanting to sponsor it...wanting me to tell him more over dinner on his yacht... Then 'accidentally' bumping into me at the Ashmolean, taking me for tea, visiting Blenheim together. And then that college dinner, where he 'just happened' to need a plus one—and needed another oh-so-convenient plus one at that Art Deco dinner-dance at the Viscari in London, dressing me up so that I was a fitting partner for him...someone a man like him would want to be seen with. And then—

Pain like a knife thrust into her.

Then taking me to bed...

For one reason only. The reason that had been slammed into her face that nightmare evening in Athens.

To get at my father...ruin his plans.

The pain of the knowledge forced upon her by her father was unbearable.

But I deserve it—I deserve it.

She deserved every last bit of the agony inside her.

'Darling?'

Her mother's voice came from the lower deck. It was full of concern. Concern that had been there since Kassia had thrown herself into her arms, swamping her petite frame, and burst into unstoppable tears. Despite her diminutive height, her mother had hugged her tightly. And now, days after she'd landed in Malaga from Amsterdam, following her desperate plea, her usually insouciant mother had gone into full maternal support role.

Kassia was abjectly grateful. She had never envisaged her butterfly mother being so full of feeling for her daughter's misery.

Kassia heard her footsteps coming up the stairs. 'Oh, darling...' she said again, pity in her voice.

Her mother, supple from all the Pilates classes Kassia knew she did to keep her figure trim, limbered down beside her onto a cushion. She helped herself to one of her daughter's hands, chafing it comfortingly.

'It will pass,' she said. 'I promise you, it will pass.' She drew back a little. 'Come and have some lunch,' she said. 'John's gone off in the launch—he and the first mate are after catching something big and inedible. It will probably take them all day. Goodness knows what the appeal of fishing is!'

Memory seared in Kassia… Damos learning how to fly-fish from Duncan MacFadyen, her sitting on the rug on the bank, watching him…

Loving him…

Her throat closed painfully, as if trying to stifle the word. How could she bear to hear it…think it…feel it? She wanted to silence it, deny it, thrust it from her. But she couldn't. That was the agony of it all…she couldn't…

Because that's what it was—I realise it now. I went and fell in love with him. I didn't know it, and didn't realise it, and now…

Now she was left with it—trapped with it. Imprisoned with it. And it was the worst thing possible.

To love a man who could use me like that. Oh, dear God, fool that I was! That I am. Fool, fool, fool!

A sob rose again, but she stifled it. Her mother had made such an effort for her, telling her to come straight to Spain, that she would be safe here, out on the yacht they'd hired, sailing off the coast.

Kassia knew from Dr Michaelis, who was so kindly allowing her indefinite leave, and from her mother's housekeeper in the Cotswolds, that Damos was trying to find her. Emotion twisted inside her, like painful cords tightening.

Heavily, she got to her feet, following her mother down to the main deck. The stewards had set the table for lunch, and memory knifed through her yet again. Of that very first evening with Damos. Aboard his yacht. When she had been tasked to do her best to persuade him to sponsor the excavation.

Her throat constricted.

All fake. All totally fake.

It hadn't been the excavation that he was interested in, that had brought him to the island.

It was me. He needed to get to meet me—it was a pretext, that was all.

A pretext that had gone on and on...

Until he had me where he wanted me.

In his bed. Ready to be paraded in front of her father.

Damos Kallinikos's latest squeeze. His latest bed warmer. Whom Cosmo Palandrou would never touch with a bargepole, so he'd walk away from doing any kind of business deal with her father. Leaving the coast clear for Damos to make his own move on Cosmo's company.

The only thing he was ever interested in...

Misery twisted again. And self-condemnation. And bitterness...

Dimly, she became aware that the captain had come down from the bridge and was addressing her mother.

'I do apologise,' he was saying, 'but I'm afraid we've been summoned back to port tomorrow. The owner requires the immediate use of a yacht—this particular one. You will be upgraded to a more expensive charter—gratis, of course—to continue your cruise.'

Her mother looked harassed, but could only comply.

And the next day, as the yacht nosed its way into the marina, its owner was waiting on the quay.

It was Damos.

Damos's expression was grim. Finally he had tracked down Kassia. Discovering that the yacht her mother and stepfather had chartered was one of his own had been the only piece of good fortune afforded him. He had recalled it immediately.

Kassia was on board—he knew that from the yacht's captain—and now she was clearly visible on deck as the yacht moored. He was seeing her again for the first time since she had fled from him that nightmare evening in Athens. He felt emotion kick in him—powerful emotion. Painful emotion…

As mooring was completed he walked up to the lowered gangplank. Kassia was as white as a sheet.

'I would like to talk to you, Kassia,' he said.

He kept his voice neutral, but the emotion that was as painful as it was powerful kicked in him again.

She didn't answer. Her mother did.

Barely touching her daughter's shoulder, Kassia's mother was indeed petite, with coiffed, tinted hair, a skilfully made-up face, and she was wearing exactly the kind of very expensive casual-chic yacht-wear that perfectly set off her trim, well-preserved figure.

Absently, he found himself realising just why Kassia—so tall, so racehorse-slender—had always compared herself so unfavourably to her mother, thereby excluding herself from any claim to beauty just because she was not like her mother in looks.

'My daughter has nothing to say to you, Mr Kallinikos,' Kassia's mother said crisply.

Damos's mouth tightened. 'But I have things that need to be said to her. Kassia?' He addressed her directly now. 'Please let me simply talk to you—that is all.' He paused. 'We can't leave it like this.'

He saw her whiten even more, but hesitate. Her mother murmured something to her and she seemed to tremble. Then, lifting her chin, she looked at him.

'Outside. At that café over there.'

She nodded towards one of the many cafés and restaurants lining the busy marina. It was the one closest to the yacht—her mother would be able to see them if they sat outside, Damos realised.

He gave a curt nod. Tension was racking through him.

He watched her walk down the gangplank, step past him. He caught a faint scent of her perfume and memory rushed back. Memory he had to thrust away. Not indulge...

She walked swiftly to the café across the cobbled stones of the quayside, and sat herself down at a table. Damos did likewise. A waiter came by and Damos ordered black coffee for himself and white for her. He knew her taste in coffee. Knew so much about her.

But not how she was going to respond to him now.

She wasn't looking at him—wasn't making eye contact. Her breathing was laboured, he could tell, and her expression tense.

The coffee arrived...the waiter disappeared. Damos began.

'We can't leave it the way it is, Kassia,' he said. His voice was low, intense. 'I have to try...try and make my peace with you.'

He sounded stilted, he knew. And he knew the words were inadequate. But they were all he had now...the only way he could express what he wanted to achieve. And so much depended on them—on what he was going to say now.

He felt emotion trying to rise up in him, but he crushed it back down. It would get in the way—complicate matters. And right now the matter was very simple. Brutally simple.

I want her back.

But even as he thought it he changed it. No, he did not *want* Kassia back.

I need her back—because without her my life is...

Unthinkable.

That was what these frantic days of trying to find her had shown him...shown him with all the tenderness of a fist slamming into his solar plexus. Over and over again.

'Peace?'

There was incredulity in her voice. She was staring at him. Now she was making eye contact—and he could almost wish she was not.

'Peace?' she said again. 'You did what you did to me and you think we can make *peace* over it?'

'I have to try, Kassia—' he began.

But she cut across him. 'Try what? Try to tell me that you *didn't* use me to get at my father? Try to tell me that everything that happened between us *wasn't* a lie from the very first? Are you going to try and deny that? You lined me up from start to finish! Knowing exactly what you were doing!'

He tried to interrupt but she would not let him. Vehemence was in her face, in her voice.

'You turned up at the excavation deliberately—are you doing to claim you didn't? And you got me to come to dinner on your yacht deliberately—are you going to deny that too? As for Oxford...' A choke broke from her. 'I thought it was a coincidence! Bumping into you like that. But it wasn't, was it? *Was it?*'

He drew a breath, his face as tight as if it were made of wire. 'No. But—'

She wouldn't let him speak.

'And after that it was easy, wasn't it? So damn easy. Spending time with me…coming up with one reason after another to do so. Reeling me in until you had me exactly where you needed me to be.' Her face contorted. 'In your bed.'

The bitterness in her voice was acid on his skin. Her eyes like knives plunging into his flesh.

'And then you could do what you'd intended to do right from the very start—make me a weapon to use against my father.' Her voice twisted. 'For money. For profit.'

Her eyes were on him still, but now there was a bleakness in them that struck him like a blow. And she struck him another blow with her next words, cutting him to the very quick.

'You once told me that there was a difference between using opportunities that presented themselves and using people to achieve them.' Her voice was hollow. 'But that wasn't a difference *you* took any notice of. I was an opportunity presenting itself to you and you took full advantage. You lied to me…made a fool of me…used me.'

She pushed her chair back, got to her feet. She looked down at him. Spoke again. But now her voice was hard. As hard as her expression. As hard as the look in her eyes.

'I thought you were different from my father, not cut from the same vile cloth.' She drew a breath, and he heard it rasp in her throat. 'How wrong I was.'

She turned away and walked back to the yacht, coffee untouched. There was something about the way she was walking, about the way her shoulders were hunching, her head dropping. He launched to his feet—then realised he had to pay for the undrunk coffee. He snatched out his wallet and dropped a note on the table, then strode after her rapidly.

He had to catch up with her.

Had to tell her what he had flown to Spain to tell her— what he would cross the world to tell her.

If she would let him…

She gained the gangplank and ran up it, head still bowed.

Someone stepped into his path. Not her mother, but her stepfather.

'Stay away from her, Mr Kallinikos. You've done quite enough damage. Leave our family alone.'

He spoke calmly, but with the authority of his years, of his place as Kassia's guardian right now. Keeping her safe from men who made use of her…

Damos looked past him. A taxi was pulling up on the quayside. Kassia and her mother were walking down the gangplank. Kassia's mother had her arm protectively around her daughter, despite the disparity in their heights. Kassia's head was turned away from him. A steward was following them with their suitcases.

Kassia's stepfather had gone to open the door of the taxi, ushering in his wife and stepdaughter. The steward put the suitcases in the boot, and Kassia's stepfather got into the front passenger seat.

The taxi moved off. Damos watched it go.

Then the taxi turned out of the marina into the traffic.
Lost to sight.

Like Kassia—lost.

Damos went on staring. Though his eyes were blind.

CHAPTER TWELVE

KASSIA POSITIONED THE tip of her trowel over the protruding shard. She had to work carefully. And work she must. Without work she could not exist. Without work she would be a ghost. Without work she would be defenceless. Work could fill her days, her mind, her thoughts.

But it could not fill her nights.

That was the time she dreaded—feared. Nights brought thoughts, and thoughts brought memories, and memories brought dreams.

And dreams brought nightmares…

Her brow furrowed now, as she teased the earth from the shard. This was the last day of the dig and she wanted to get this shard out—and those that went with it. She was the last person in the trench, for the site was being shut down for overwintering. All the finds were packed away, all the notes and catalogues boxed up to be taken back to the museum. Her winter would be filled with completing the work done so far—typing up the paperwork, getting restoration work underway in the lab, choosing what should go on display, what should be sent to other museums, what archived.

Winter would keep her busy. And that was essential.

How long ago summer was. It was late autumn now, and

the weather was breaking. Rain squalls were not uncommon, and a chill wind was sweeping down off the steppes. Time to hunker down…stay warm and dry.

Memory pierced… She and Damos, lolling by the roaring fire in the castle in the Highlands, rain spattering on the leaded windows, and she and he playing chess. Her mouth twisted and she dug the tip of her trowel in with more ferocity than she should. Damos had run circles around her playing chess. Just as he'd run circles around her in all the time he'd spent with her. Right from the very start.

She lifted her head. This trench, deserted but for herself, was an extension of where she'd been working all those months ago—the first time she had ever set eyes on Damos Kallinikos.

She felt her vision smear and dropped her head again. Her hand gripped the trowel so tightly her earth-stained hands went white. Dimly, she heard voices nearby, but her vision was still smeared.

Then someone tapped her hesitantly on the shoulder. She started, looking up. It was Dr Michaelis. But it was not only him she saw. It was the man behind him.

Damos.

Was he insane? The words were inside Damos's head, but it was as if he could hear them audibly. Insane to come here? Hadn't Spain taught him his lesson?

She wants nothing to do with me—nothing.

Yet he was here, all the same. Two months on. Months that had been like nothing he had ever endured in his life. Months that had made those brief weeks in the summer seem like a distant, impossible dream—a dream to torment him and torture him. For it was lost to him for ever.

As Kassia was lost to him.

Pain buckled through him at the knowledge of what he had done.

Everything she told me I had.

As he stood there now, looking down at Kassia hunkered in the trench, a terrible sense of *déjà vu* came over him. It was as if time were collapsing and he was seeing her as he had seen her for the very first time.

He felt a vice around his chest, tightening pitilessly.

But he deserved no pity…

Deserved only the pain that was now his constant companion.

Dr Michaelis was addressing her, and Damos could hear the awkwardness in his voice. He felt bad for him, but his need was too great. Too desperate.

'Ah, Kassia… Kyrios Kallinikos has…has asked the favour of a word with you.'

Kassia's expression did not change. Nor did she look at Damos. She got to her feet. She said nothing—only stepped out of the trench.

'Good, good…' said Dr Michaelis, sounding flustered. He hurried away.

Kassia's eyes went to Damos. There was something wrong with them, he could see. They looked…*smeared.*

She still didn't speak—just stood there. Memory poured through him. He could swear she was wearing the same earth-coloured baggy cotton trousers, the same mustard-coloured tee—though this time she wore a tan gilet over it against the chillier weather. Her hair was screwed up in a careless knot on her head, and she wore not a scrap of make-up—unless he counted the flecks of dirt on her cheeks.

The memory struck at him of how she'd walked back to the yacht at the marina in Spain, her shoulders hunched, head down. All the confidence that she'd glowed with once he'd got her to realise just how beautiful she was had gone. As if it had never been…

She was still not speaking, only looking at him with those smeared, blank eyes.

He made himself speak. Say what he had come here to say.

'I… I have something that I would like to tell you. That I… I would like you to know.'

His voice was hesitant—but how should it not be? Twice already she had not let him speak—in Athens and in Spain.

'I… I wanted you to know that I have been funding the museum. Your father…' his voice was strained '…withdrew his support after—'

He broke off, then made himself continue.

'I did not want the museum to suffer, so I stepped in. It was…something I could do. But I don't…don't say this in any expectation that you might…might think less ill of me—'

He broke off again. Those blank, smeared eyes conveyed nothing. Nor did she say anything.

He went on with what he had come here to say.

'My acquisition of Cosmo Palandrou's company has gone through—I used a proxy, whom I funded, who then sold it on to me. It had been badly mismanaged, and industrial disputes were endemic. Since my acquisition I have created an employee share scheme which allocates half the company to all the employees, at no cost to themselves. Profits will be shared fifty-fifty, and my share will be re-invested for the company's expansion. I,' he added, 'will not be benefitting financially.'

He stopped. What he had to say next was hardest of all. But he must say it. Even though Kassia still had not moved, her blank smeared gaze was still on him.

'I have done this because you told me in Spain that I had used you to make money for myself.'

His face contorted suddenly. Something broke inside him.

'Oh, God, Kassia, if only I could undo what I did to you! I regret it so, so much! But I can't undo it. All I can do is live with the consequences. Live with what I have lost.'

His voice dropped. There was a stone in his throat, making it impossible to breathe. To speak. But he must speak. Must say the most agonising words in the world.

'You,' he said. 'I have lost you.'

He turned to go. She was still motionless, still unspeaking, not reacting. There was no point in him staying here. No point at all…

But as he started to turn away he saw something happen to her face. Rivulets of tears were running down it…

The tears were spilling. She could not stop them. No power on earth could stop them.

'Kassia—'

Her name was on his lips. And then his arms were around her.

She should pull away—push him away, drive him away,

force him away. For he was the man who had lied to her from the very first moment she had ever seen him, standing right here. Standing here, planning to lie to her, to make use of her, to make her the gullible, stupid fool her father had called her in his rage.

She should push him from her—but she did not. Could not.

His arms were holding her, cradling her. She heard his voice.

'Don't cry. Don't weep. I beg you! I can't bear that you should weep. I can't bear that I did to you what I did! It's an agony to me.'

She was clinging to him—but why she was, she didn't know. How could she? How could she cling like this to a man who had used her as he had? Lied to her as he had?

'You lied to me Damos! You lied and you lied and you lied! Everything was a lie—all a lie! Every day we had together. Every hour. Every night in your arms.' Her voice choked, sobs racking her. 'It was all a *lie*!'

She felt his arms stiffen. Then they fell away, dropping to his sides. He let her go and looked away, out over the deserted trenches to the olive trees beyond. Then his eyes came back to hers. Held them fast.

'It started as a lie,' he said.

He paused, and the silence between them stretched like a chasm. Then he spoke again, his eyes still holding hers fast.

'But it became the truth,' he said.

He heard the words he had said. The words that were the most important words in the world.

'It became the truth,' he said again.

His eyes searched her face. He could read nothing there. Nothing to help him. But he did not deserve help.

After all that had been a lie between them she deserved the truth. The truth about the truth.

'The truth is brutal. Everything you threw at me in Spain—that I engineered meeting you, feigning an interest in sponsoring the dig, and invited you on board my yacht on that pretext…that I found out you were attending a conference in Oxford, so I turned up there myself, letting you think it was just by chance. I kept our acquaintance going, knowing exactly where I wanted it to lead. Knowing exactly why I was doing it. But then…then it changed.'

He knew his face was stark.

'It changed, Kassia. I realised I was enjoying your company…that I wanted more of it. That I wanted Kassia—*you*. Not Kassia Andrakis, who was going to be the means by which I would outmanoeuvre your father, but you. Just you. For who you were yourself. I wanted you—I wanted to spend time with you—I wanted to be with you. And above all…' his voice changed now, and there was a husk in it that he could not hide '…I wanted you in my arms.'

He shut his eyes for a moment. Then flared them open.

'Oh, God, Kassia, how much I wanted that! And I wanted you to want it too! And the more I found out about you—how you lacked any confidence in your own beauty, which you could not see—the more I wanted to reveal it to you. And I did—I did just that! And when…when we came together that night, I knew I had found someone.' His voice dropped, 'Someone I did not want to lose.'

He drew a breath. Words were still coming—the truth was still coming.

'Our time in the Highlands was the most precious time in my life. I felt a happiness I had never known before, being with you. We were good together—so very, very good. And I knew it was the same for you. I knew then that I did not want to be without you. I wanted our time together to go on, back here in Greece, just as I told you. But then—'

He broke off. Shut his eyes again for a moment, unable to bear seeing her looking at him. But he must bear it—must bear what he now had to say.

'I had to deal with what I had set up when I first came here. The plan to…to use you for my own ends. If…if there had been more time I'd have wanted us simply to be seen in Athens as a couple. The news would soon have reached Cosmo and your father. But there wasn't time for that. So I… I decided I just wanted it over and done with—the whole damn thing. I wanted to force the issue…have Cosmo and your father presented with us together and that would end it. I just didn't realise…'

He stopped again.

'It horrified me,' he said at last. 'Appalled me. What your father said to you.' His voice dropped. 'And it appalled me that I had exposed you to it—to that vile diatribe from your father…saying such things to you.'

He swallowed. There was a razor in his throat, but he swallowed anyway. He had no choice but to do so. He was telling her the truth about the truth.

'But I exposed myself as well. Exposed myself to your father's accusation of me. That I had used you.' He stopped again, then went on, making himself speak. His voice was low and drawn. 'I hadn't wanted you ever to know…to know that I had come here deliberately, wanting to use you.

Oh, I'd told myself at the start, when I dreamt up the idea,
that it would do you no harm, my taking an interest in you.
That if you did not want to get involved with me then that
would be that. And if you did, you would likely enjoy your
time with me because—well, why not? I even told myself
that since you couldn't possibly *want* Cosmo Palandrou
foisted on you—what woman would?—you might appreciate the impact of our affair yourself. I told myself all that...'

He took another breath, ragged and razored.

'But when I realised that I wanted you for yourself, not
for any other reason...then I didn't know what to do. I felt
an impulse to come clean—to tell you why I had originally
sought you out. But then I hesitated. It was too risky. It was
safer not to tell you. I thought you need never know, because
by then it did not matter. I wanted you for yourself, for real,
and what we had together was so very precious to me, becoming more precious still with every day that passed. So
why tell you anything about my original intentions?'

He stopped, his eyes veiled.

'But there was another reason I did not want to tell
you—a reason I did not want to face. But in Spain you
made me face it.'

He looked away, out over the serried trenches to the
olive trees beyond. When his eyes came back to her they
were bleak.

'In Spain, you told me I was exactly like your father—
using other people for my own ends, as I had used you. And
it shamed me—I deserved it to shame me.'

His eyes were bleaker still. Bleak as a polar waste where
no warmth could ever come. His voice was just as bleak.

'But I am paying the price now, Kassia. Believe me, if

you believe nothing else, I *am* paying the price. It's a price I deserve to pay for what I did. And it is a price I would not wish on anyone. I have lost you, and I cannot bear it. Except I know I must.'

I must bear this unbearable loss because I made it happen myself. And nothing can undo it—nothing.

Emotion speared him, right in his guts, twisting viciously. He had to bear that too...

He turned away. There was no point being here any longer. He had to go and live without her, all his days.

A hand touched his arm. Kassia's hand. And then there was Kassia's voice, speaking low and faint.

'Don't go,' she said. Her voice was almost inaudible. 'Don't go,' she said again. 'Don't leave me.'

His face stilled. His breath stilled. The world stilled.

He looked round at her. She wasn't looking at him. Her head was bowed, shoulders hunched.

'Don't leave me,' she said again. A husk...a whisper. 'I can't bear for you to leave me. I don't want to lose you. I lost you before, and I can't bear to lose you again. Not now...'

He heard her words but he did not believe them—dared not believe them. Dared not. And yet...

Slowly, he turned. The touch of her hand on his sleeve was so faint it was scarcely there at all. But he felt it tremble, as if it might fall from him at any moment.

She lifted her head now. What was in her eyes, he did not know. And yet he must speak. His heart seemed to be filling his chest.

'Don't say that,' he breathed, 'if you do not mean it.'

She shook her head. Slowly. As if she were moving it

against the weight of the world. Against the weight of what
he had done to her.

A rasp sounded in his throat, torn from his stricken
lungs.

There was urgency in his words. 'Kassia, if you will
have me after all I've done to you, what I would give all
the world to undo, I would beg your forgiveness—but how
can you forgive me?'

She lifted her other hand, and with a touch that was as
light as the hand on his sleeve she brushed his cheek.

'But I do,' she whispered.

Her eyes were lifted to his, and he saw they were no
longer smeared, but lit with a silver light.

'Kassia, dear God... *Kassia!*'

That emotion was sweeping up in him, powerful and
strange and unknown—the emotion that had swept over
him the night he had made Kassia his own. But now he
knew what it was. Knew that the spear which had been
thrust so deep inside him, twisting viciously as he'd faced
walking away from her for ever, was suddenly gone.

With a jerking movement he folded his hand over hers
on his sleeve. Pressed it down. Never to let it go. Never...

Then he slipped his fingers under hers. Lifted them.
Lifted them to his mouth. Kissed them.

In homage and in plea—and in love.

Because that was what he knew was filling him—that
was what had caused that unbearable sense of loss when
she had fled from him that hideous night. That had been
the desperation driving him to find her, to make his confession to her, to do whatever he could to make amends.

To show her that what had started as a lie had become the truth…to beg her to believe him.

'I am yours,' he said, and his voice was low, filled with all he felt, all he had come to feel, would always feel. 'I am yours for however long you might want me. Yours for an hour, or a day, or a single night—or for a lifetime.'

She reached up a hand, enfolded his as it enfolded hers. She was looking at him now, and her eyes were filling again with tears. But her tears were diamonds…

'Or for eternity?' she said, and reached his lips with hers.

Was this love? Was this love pouring through her like a tide? Washing away all that had tarnished and poisoned and destroyed? Was it love she had tried to silence, to kill, after she'd realised what he'd done to her?

Oh, but it must be love! For what else could lift her like this? What else could turn agony and anguish into such joy? Such joy as streamed through her?

He was sweeping her to him, crushing her to him, saying her name, kissing her hair, her cheek, her mouth.

'I don't deserve you—I don't deserve a single hair on your head. I don't deserve a single moment with you! Oh, God, Kassia, if only I could undo—'

She pulled away—but only to place a finger across his mouth, to silence him.

'No more,' she whispered. 'It's gone…it's over—we will never let it come between us again. Simply to know how much you regret it means all the world to me. It…it heals us, Damos. Heals all the harm that was done.'

She kissed him again, to seal that healing. And then, as

she drew back, she spoke again. There was something new in her voice now. A rueful note.

'And you know…maybe we should be grateful for your coming here for the reason you did. Because if you hadn't… would we ever have met? And if we had—in Athens, say— you would have had some gorgeous, glamorous female with you and you would not have looked twice at me.'

She was given no chance to say more. Words fell from him, urgent and vehement.

'Kassia, if you spend the rest of your life looking exactly as you do now, without a scrap of make-up and in clothes that should be buried deeper than those broken pots you keep digging up, I will love you and adore you and desire you all the rest of my days!'

He seized her hands, his eyes pouring into hers, and what she saw in them made her faint with love.

'It's *you* whom I love! And when I say I will always, *always* want you to look as stunning as I know you can, it is for *you*—not me!'

His mouth lowered to hers, and in the touch of his lips was all that she could ever desire. For a long time they kissed, and as at last they drew apart she saw he was gazing down at her, love light in his eyes…love light that was like a warming flame inside her, one that would warm her all her days, and all her nights, for ever and for good.

Her heart was singing. It would sing for ever now.

Damos's arms came around her and he held her close, against his heart, where now she would always be. Her arms wrapped him just as close, and closer still. Heart against heart—for all eternity indeed. And so much longer.

EPILOGUE

KASSIA COULDN'T STOP LAUGHING. Both she and Damos were making endless mistakes, but no one minded. All the other dancers were helpfully calling out to them which way they should be turning, whose hands they should be taking now. One thing was for sure, though, reeling was an energetic business. The foot-tapping music was driving them on, with fiddles, pipes, drums and accordions, and it was just impossible not to dance. They'd already Stripped the Willow, Dashed the White Sergeant, been to Mairi's Wedding, and were now completely confused in an eightsome reel.

When it ended she was more than ready to collapse down on one of the chairs around the edge of the village hall where the *ceilidh* was being held.

'Not bad, lassie…not bad at all.'

Duncan MacFadyen, looking not out of breath in the slightest, came up to her. He looked resplendent in his fil-ibeg short kilt, simply worn with a white shirt and tie. His nephew was the piper in the band, and Mrs MacFadyen was presiding over the groaning supper table.

Damos came up too. He also looked not out of breath in the slightest.

Duncan clapped him on the shoulder. 'We'll make a Scotsman out of you yet, laddie,' he said approvingly.

Damos laughed. 'Kassia and I will practise in Greece in time for our visit in the summer,' he promised.

He'd procured a glass of beer for himself and Duncan, and presented Kassia with a glass of cider—which she knocked back thirstily.

'We'll be a respectable married couple by then, Duncan,' she said.

'So we're making the most of our last illicit romantic getaway here,' Damos said, with a glint in his eye.

'Och, well, winter's as good a time as any for keeping warm together,' Duncan chuckled with cheerful wickedness.

Kassia smiled, thinking of how very, very warm Damos kept her in the velvet-hung four-poster in the castle bedroom. She and Damos, after a Christmas spent with Kassia's mother and stepfather, hadn't been able to resist taking a Hogmanay break back here.

In the castle where we fell in love.

And where they'd be spending their honeymoon, too, next summer.

It was a long time to wait—but Kassia could not deprive her mother of the pleasure of organising a huge, full-works traditional wedding for them, with a reception at her stepfather's country house in the Cotswolds. There would be a marquee on the lawn, a lavish wedding breakfast, and dancing under the stars in the evening.

Her mother was in her element, and Kassia was giving her her head, knowing how much her social butterfly mother was enjoying it. As for herself—she'd have been just as happy taking her vows simply by hand-fasting, in the centuries-old Scottish union of those who loved each other, holding Damos's hand, quietly and on their own.

Perhaps that was what they would do. Walk down to the edge of the loch while they were here—warmly wrapped against the Scottish winter. Or perhaps at the summit of the Munro that Damos was determined to bag before they flew home. He'd already made the outdoor wear shopkeeper in Inverlochry an even happier man by taking Kassia there and kitting them out with winter walking gear.

'We'll bag our second Munro now,' he'd said. 'A nice easy one for winter walking. And then try a tougher one in the summer. And we'll keep going from there, doing another couple every annual visit, until we've bagged the lot!'

Kassia had laughed. 'There are close on three hundred!' she'd exclaimed.

Damos had dropped a kiss on her forehead. 'Well, maybe we'll settle for half. And that...' he'd taken her hand, his eyes warm upon her '...should see us into ripe old age. We might even still be tottering up them when we reach our centenaries!'

Kassia had squeezed his hand. That she and he should be granted so long a time together was all her heart's desire. She'd felt her heart swell then, and it was doing so again now, as she gazed up at Damos as he downed his beer, so tall, so gorgeous, and so infinitely dear to her.

How much I love him—how very, very much.

After their rapturous reconciliation everything had been so simple. Dr Michaelis had given her extra leave on the spot, and she and Damos had flown back to Athens, wrapped in each other's arms. They'd spent the weekend at his apartment in Piraeus, barely surfacing, and then he'd come with her to England. He had made his peace with her mother and shaken her stepfather's hand.

There was only one hand he could not, *would* not shake. Nor would Kassia ever expect it of him. Or of herself. Her break with her father was absolute—it could not be otherwise. And though it cast a shadow over her it was one she would not let blight her. It would be her stepfather who would give her away at her wedding.

Till then, she and Damos were doing what he had suggested to her when they'd left the castle in the summer. She could not let Dr Michaelis down, so would continue at the museum until her wedding, contenting herself with weekends with Damos. Then, once married, she would seek a post in Athens.

But it might not last that long. Already Damos was hinting.

'This apartment is all very well for the two of us, but it wouldn't suit a family,' he'd declared.

'But let's enjoy some time together first as a couple,' Kassia had said. 'Doing all the things you've promised me you'll do.'

Damos was stepping back from many of his business concerns. He had sold his yacht charter company, and was divesting himself of some of his merchant marine interests. And he had decided, once Cosmo Palandrou's freight and logistics business was in good order, to reduce his share even more.

'I want to enjoy life,' he'd said to Kassia. 'Learn scuba diving…go sailing with you…travel more. Our time together has taught me that.'

'I'm glad,' she'd said. 'You've worked so hard, Damos, to get where you are today—now relax, and enjoy the fruits of all your hard work. After all...' she'd given him a wry, quizzical look '...one day we'll be like all those souls who lived three thousand years ago in the Bronze Age, with the archaeologists of the future digging up the remnants of our lives, wondering what they were like. So...' she'd kissed him on the cheek '...let's make sure they are *good* lives.'

They were words that came to her again now, as the band struck up once more. Immediately her foot started tapping irresistibly.

Damos finished his beer and took her empty cider glass from her, placing both on the windowsill behind her chair.

'Away with you both now,' Duncan said jovially. 'Back to the *ceilidh*.'

He packed them off back to the dance floor. And as she and Damos took their places memory struck her.

'Do you realise,' she said, 'that this evening is the first time we've danced together since that night at the Viscari?'

She felt her heart swell again. The memory was sweet, so very sweet, and that night had started the affair that now would be their marriage, all their lives, for ever and beyond.

Her eyes went to Damos now, as they stood opposite each other, waiting their turn. He met her eyes full on, and in them was such a blaze of love that it made her reel.

And then the reeling was for real...

'It's you!' the woman next to her said.

Kassia started forward, and Damos did too, seizing her

hand. Hand in hand, their eyes still locked together, they went down the line, hand-fasted, heart-fasted, united in their love for each other, dancing into the future that was theirs and theirs alone.

And always would be.

* * * * *

If you just couldn't get enough of
Vows of Revenge
then be sure to check out these other dramatic stories
by Julia James!

The Cost of Cinderella's Confession
Reclaimed by His Billion-Dollar Ring
Contracted as the Italian's Bride
The Heir She Kept from the Billionaire
Greek's Temporary Cinderella

Available now!